'HE CAME, HE SAW, HE CONKED US'!

ANCIENT ADVENTURES

SCOTTISH SAGAS

Edited By Rob Harding

Years of YoungWriters

First published in Great Britain in 2016 by:

Coltsfoot Drive
Peterborough
PE2 9BF
Telephone: 01733 890066
Website: www.youngwriters.co.uk

FOREWORD

Welcome to 'Ancient Adventures – Scottish Sagas'.

Can you imagine reliving exciting tales from the past? What might it have been like to experience some of history's most important events? Well, telling those stories is precisely what the writers of this collection have done. Inside you will find work by 7-11-year-olds from across Scotland.

Their stories cover everything from the terrible sinking of the Titanic to the gruesome rituals of the Aztecs, what it meant to be a king's Groom of the Throne, how king Tutankhamun may have planned to murder Cleopatra and lots more in between. You'll find plenty of laughter, heartbreak, terror and adventures waiting inside, as well as a handful of Vikings, mummies, kings, queens and dinosaurs.

Strap in and get ready to travel through time and space with these fantastic Ancient Adventures.

Rob Harding

CONTENTS

Estelle Murray (10)	22
Morven Pennington (10)	22
Grace Brogan (10)	23
Scott McBride (10)	23
Rob Miller (11)	24
Reece Denham (10)	24
Jack Morris (10)	25
Struan Thomson (11)	25
Nina Porter (10)	26
Millie Woods (10)	26
Amy Mitchell (11)	27
Callum Pennington (9)	27
Abbie Curran (10)	28
Sophie Blackmore (10)	28

Eoligarry Primary School, Isle Of Barra

Domhnall Douglas	29
Darren MacNeil (9)	30

Hallglen Primary School, Falkirk

Sophie Mitchell (8)	31
Douglas Stephen (8)	31
Abby Rose Honeyman (8)	32
Fraser Christie (11)	32
Ashleigh Elizabeth Wilson (11)	33
Kelsie Middleton (8)	33
Jack Aitchison (8)	34
Wiktoria Kaleta (8)	34
Kyle Cringean (9)	35
Mia Ann Tracey (8)	35
Mckenzie Craig (8)	36
Arran Richardson (8)	36
Emma-Louise Ferrier (8)	37
Lucas Beck (9)	37
Ella Gibson (7)	38

Nicole Claire Padkin (8)	38
Hope Griffin (11)	39
Regan Grierson (8)	40
Eilidh Thomson (8)	40
Nathan Walker (8)	41
Ruby McNamee (8)	41

Hamnavoe Primary School, Shetland

Connor Jackson (10)	42
Elise Rendall (9)	42
Caitlin Kok (9)	43
Logan Tait (10)	43
Lewis Drever	44
Keegan Brown (10)	44
Ellis Young (9)	45

Kenmore Primary School, Aberfeldy

India Ross (9)	46
Aileen Sporleder (8)	46
Murray Weir (8)	47
Max England (7)	47
Annie Dott (7)	48
Adam Hitchins (9)	48
Cameron Kimpton (8)	49

Lochmaddy Primary School, Isle Of North Uist

Jack MacDonald (8)	50
Andrew MacDonald (11)	50
Charlie MacDonald (10)	51
Anna MacDonald (9)	51
Blair MacKenzie (8)	52
Katie MacAulay (10)	52
Rachel Morrison (11)	53

Longforgan Primary School, Dundee

Grace Berry (10)	54
Campbell Thomson (10)	54
Adam Laing (10)	55
Ruby Blackmore (11)	55
Logan James Roy Soutar (10)	56
Orla Stewart (11)	56
Caelan Milne (11)	57
Amy Johnston (9)	57
Georgia Thomson (9)	58
Emma Henderson (10)	58
Callum Bradley (9)	59
Grace Prest (9)	59
Sahar Jafferbhoy (10)	60
Niamh McMahon (11)	60
Reuben McCulloch (10)	61
Lucy Stoves (9)	61
Owen Smith (10)	62
Ailidh Milne (10)	62
Eve Stewart (9)	63
Fraser Johnston (9)	63
Abbey Mailley (10)	64

Loretto Junior School, Musselburgh

Áine Coad (11)	65
Evie McNamara (10)	65
Yassin Shaker (8)	66
Michael Williams (11)	66
Tom Shanks (10)	67
Janica Chan (10)	67
Rory Kemp (10)	68
Sally Watson (10)	68
Samuel Mukherjee (10)	69
Eleanor Talbot (11)	69
Oliver Mukherjee (10)	70

Jamie Barker (9)	70
Imaan Zaidi (8)	71
Grace Crawford (9)	71
Rory Lang (8)	72
Ollie Shanks (8)	72

Meethill School, Peterhead

Morgan Forgie (7)	73
Olek Kulczyk (9)	73
Evangeline Vanwyk (7)	74
Ryan Dow (8)	74
Erica-Leigh Davidson (8)	75
Danielius Babicius (8)	75
Nicole McGee (8)	76
Megan Ovenstone (7)	76
Chloe Plant (8)	77

Mosstodloch Primary School, Fochabers

Cerys Stuart (10)	78

Our Lady's RC Primary School, Perth

Magnus Campbell (11)	79
Dominic Bews (10)	79

Riverside Primary School, Stirling

Karol Wieliczko (10)	80
Jack Allan (10)	80
Finlay Barr (10)	81
Erin Spence (10)	81
& Katie Reilly (10)	

Sound Primary School, Shetland

Dannika Leask (11)	82
Kara Grant (11)	82
Lucy Kerr (11)	83
Keegan Watt (11)	83
Dylan Hunter (11)	84
Jack Duncan (11)	84
Ally Morrison (10)	85
Fern Semple (10)	85
Lulu Johnson (10)	86
Ciaran Leask (12)	86
Jenna Black (11)	87
Isla Murphy (12)	87
Jordan Leask (12)	88
Wayne Leask (12)	88
Matthew Spence (11)	89
Lotti Rendall (11)	89
Estella Smith (11)	90
Ellie Bisset (11)	90
Zoe Semple (11)	91
Freya Laurenson (11)	91
Xander Souter (12)	92
Vinessa Carr	92
Tahlia Leslie (11)	93
Jessie Jamieson (10)	93
Laura Bisset (11)	94
Laurie Morris (11)	94
Sarah Louise McAllister (12)	95
Ryan Peart (11)	95
Emma Leask (12)	96
Johnathan Goudie (11)	97
Ethan Dunn (10)	97
Christian Thomas Anderson (10)	98
Eve Fraser (10)	98
Finn Regan (10)	99
Liam Robbie Slater (10)	99

Hayley Moar (11)	100
Hayden Fraser (9)	101
Jason Campbell (12)	101
Eloise March (9)	102
Ellie Chapman (8)	102
Brooke Leslie (8)	103
Ashleigh Calderwood (9)	103
Adam Card (8)	104
Aaron Regler (11)	104
Sonny Teale (12)	105
Kelsey Neill (8)	105
Sebastian Nicol (8)	106
Leland Wiseman (9)	106
Koby Sinclair (8)	107
Isaac Ritchie (8)	107

St Aloysius Primary School, Airdrie

Neve Hogg (7)	108

St Anthony's Primary School, Saltcoats

Mirabelle Tipping (9)	109
Rachel McGuire (9)	109
Calum Lynch (9)	110
Abby Tolland (9)	110
Leah McColl (10)	111
Niamh Milne (9)	111

St Marie's Primary School, Kirkcaldy

Shon Thomas (11)	112
Natalia Podlesiecka (11)	112
Emily Ferguson (11)	113
Daniel Martin (11)	113
Bryony McCormick (11)	114
Evan Wishart (11)	114

Emma-Louise Nisbet (11) 115
Claire Nicholson (11) 115
Owen Thomson (11) 116
Kyle Barclay (11) 116
Owen Parry (11) 117
Mark Robertson (11) 117

Strath Of Appin Primary School, Appin

James Whitelaw (9) 118
Jenny Whitelaw (9) 118
Callan Taylor (9) 119
Duncan Cameron (8) 119
Jack Johnston (9) 120
Daisy Carmichael (8) 120
Erin Claire Jackson (8) 121
Ellie Hearnden (8) 121
Max Allen (9) 122
Eva MacColl (10) 122
Megan Currie (9) 123
Eve Lawrie (8) 123

Stromness Primary School, Stromness

David Laughton (10) 124
Eilidh Cursiter (9) 124
Sarah Loveridge (9) 125
Christy MacLeod (10) 125
Einar Towrie (10) 126
Olivia Macnamara (9) 126
Alistair Park (9) 127
Zara Johnston (9) 127
Matylda Kaluzinska (9) 128
Leah Jean Hamilton (9) 128
Ethan Kennedy (9) 129
Kayla Swannie (10) 129
James Hogg (10) 130

Jordan Gunn (9) 130
Leo Naylor (9) 131
Katrina Braddock (10) 131
Thorfinn Sinclair (9) 132
George Argo (10) 132
Holly Mae McLellan (10) 133
Taigan Adamson (9) 133
Connor Bayliss (9) 134
Ewan Foubister (10) 134

Tulloch Primary School, Perth

Fern Dickson (8) 135
Milla Craig (9) 135

Wallacestone Primary School, Falkirk

Elise Gavin (8) 136
Nathaniel Hutton (9) 136
Robbie Seaton (8) 137
Euan Menzies (8) 137
Carly Jane Crawford (8) 138
Jack Savage (8) 138
Kailim Grant (8) 139
Olivia Chomczuk (8) 139
Beth Fletcher (8) 140
Cameron McLean (8) 140
Lewis Smith (8) 141
Dean Johnston (9) 141
Cameron Hudson (8) 142
Robbie Hill (8) 142
Eva Inglis (8) 143
Finlay Christie (8) 143

THE
MINI SAGAS

Peasant To Knight

Tom walked to the castle and read the board. 'See The King's Fantastical Sapphire!' He thought it was pretty cool so he went to have a look. As he walked up to the guard he was checked to make sure he had no weapons. Tom stared around in amazement until his eyes rested on a shady figure on the chandelier. The figure took one glance in Tom's direction and shot to the throne in one great leap. It was only a matter of seconds until the gem would be gone. Tom caught the thief in a headlock. Tom got knighted!

David Dawson (11)
Aberuthven Primary School, Auchterarder

Cleopatra

Cleopatra was the Queen of Egypt. One day Cleopatra got a statue of herself.
Two hours later the servant came in. 'Your Majesty, the Vikings are attacking.' Cleopatra didn't know what to do.
'Argh! Get the guards!'
'Cleopatra, most of them are already dead.'
Now Cleopatra really didn't know what to do! 'Now what do I do?' said the queen.
'I don't know,' said the servant.
Suddenly there was a loud noise. 'What was that?' Cleopatra asked.
'I don't know,' said the servant. Cleopatra had to fight by herself. She died.

Hannah Wemyss (10)
Aberuthven Primary School, Auchterarder

The Tomb Of Lost Souls

'Help!' said Queen Lamba. Her servants rushed to her side. They asked her what was wrong. She said she was having a baby. Before they could say, 'Help us', there it was, a lovely baby girl. A few years passed, Queen Lamba snuck out one night. She went into her husband's tomb. It was wet and cold and covered with booby traps. His mummy tried to make her a mummy too. He turned into a goat. She killed the goat. Her daughter was very sad when her mother died. What happened to her? Well, that is another story.

Eleanor Kinmond (9)
Auchtergaven Primary School, Perth

The Lost Pyramid Of Egypt

One day, a man called Thomas was in a time travel machine. Then he crashed with a thud! 'Where am I?' Then he saw a pyramid so he went in. When he got there he found a room. There was a box of gold in it. Suddenly, the doors shut so he tried to smash them with some gold. It worked but then two mummies started to chase him so he ran to the time machine and he went back home.

Thomas Allan (7)
Auchtergaven Primary School, Perth

The Evil Pyramid

One day, me and Kian went into a pyramid. Kian went missing then I was running very fast. I was hiding when I saw Kian. Suddenly, there were fifty mummies. I started to run through all of them. I was going to get out of the pyramid but it was shut. All of the mummies were there. I was trapped! There was a doorway nearby. I was running away from them to get out. I hid in a tombstone from the mummies who were after me and Kian. We were safe.

Owen Bryce (8)
Auchtergaven Primary School, Perth

One Thousand Mummies

A man called Zack came back home and saw 1,000 mummies, so ran to his house. He was surrounded. He picked up a shovel and hit his way through them. He escaped and called for help. Nobody picked up the phone. They were coming to him and he ran to the mummies and tried to get them all with the shovel. He didn't get them all but he got 900 mummies; 100 mummies were still there. His friends came and they worked together and they killed them all. He felt great.

Christopher MacDougall (8)
Auchtergaven Primary School, Perth

Lost In Egypt

One day in Edinburgh, a tall man called Indiana Jones woke up. He made some jam on toast then sat on his favourite chair. *Boom!* His knife and fork in his hands, *thump*, he landed on sand. 'Wow! Now I know where Egypt is. I like Egypt,' he said. He was in a pyramid and he heard a noise. It was coming from the entrance. It was a mummy. *Zoom!* He zoomed back.
'Hi.' It was a king. *Bang!* He hit the back of a tomb. The door closed.
'I'll kick the door open.' *Bang!* 'I've opened it. Bye!'

Aaron Baker (8)
Auchtergaven Primary School, Perth

The Adventurer

An adventurer went to Egypt where there were booby traps. Suddenly, all the mummies chased the adventurer out of the pyramid. When the mummies came out of the pyramid they went on their knees and they covered their eyes because they didn't like the sun. The adventurer got away. The adventurer went to Pharaoh's castle. Suddenly, one of the guards saw the adventurer. The guard tried to kill the adventurer but he missed. Suddenly, the guard picked the adventurer up and put him in the dungeon. He didn't like the dark dungeon and tried to escape.

Hannah Dwyer (7)
Auchtergaven Primary School, Perth

The Remains Of The Egyptian Period

One night in Egypt, a hero named Boris and his hero dog, Todd, were the only two survivors to come back from World War 269537. Boris was entering his pyramid when suddenly... the evil emperor was invading. 'Run for your lives, villagers!' said Boris. 'My army will protect you.'

At the end of the war, the place was ruined. The villagers had managed to run away. Luckily, Todd had survived by hiding under a sandstone boulder. Boris' army was helping him to find Todd. So now that Todd was found, they rebuilt the place and the pyramids.

Patrick Farron (8)
Auchtergaven Primary School, Perth

The Missing Monkeys

One sunny morning, when the soldiers were getting dressed and getting their weapons, they got their monkeys and told them to pick pears and apples for their breakfast. One monkey got kidnapped by Zack the murderer. Zack was jealous that the soldiers had monkeys working for them. Nine monkeys came back. 'Where is monkey number ten?' There was silence. 'What's going on?'

They went out looking for the monkey. They heard a noise in the bushes. It was Zack with the monkey. 'Got you. You're going into jail. Hahaha! Look, he wants out.'

Charlie Norris (8)
Auchtergaven Primary School, Perth

The Explorer John

A long time ago in Egypt, an explorer called John was chasing mummies who had come back to life after being dead.

He went into a pyramid on the ground floor. In the floor were parts that activated the traps: snakes in the roof, crocodiles in the floor, arrows in the wall.

Then the explorer saw a mummy. A hundred mummies! The explorer punched and fought until he saw a giant mummy. The explorer said, 'I can never destroy this thing.' Then he punched one more time and the explorer destroyed the giant mummy.

Jorge Eslava (7)
Bridge Of Allan Primary School, Stirling

Mummy Adventure

It was a baking hot day in Egypt. I was walking next to the Great Pyramid of Giza when a mummy came out of it. I ran around Egypt but it caught me. I kicked it in the privates then ran to a weaponry store and got a sword, a bow and a quiver. Then I saw the mummy. I shot it plenty of times but it survived. Then I ran and ran but it chased me into a pyramid. It led me into a trap. I stepped on a pressure stone and the pyramid crumbled to a million pieces.

Jamie McQueen (7)
Bridge Of Allan Primary School, Stirling

Wrapped In Bandages!

One day I was walking past the pyramid collecting food for my family because my dad had a broken arm. All of a sudden a mummy came rushing out!

I tried to run but I tripped over a snake. The mummy tied me up in bandages, put me inside a sarcophagus and put it on the River Nile! Luckily, my friend was nearby and heard my calls. He saved me then the mummy slipped and drowned.

After a while I looked in the water and all that was left of the mummy was a pile of bandages.

Cassica Low (8)
Bridge Of Allan Primary School, Stirling

Horror Story

It was a really hot day in Egypt and a mummy scared the life out of me when he jumped out of the Pyramid of Giza. It had demon eyes and blood dripping from its teeth. I ran for my life. It was terrifying.

I ran around the country. The mummy fell on his face because he had got his bandages stuck in the tree and it was hilarious. He farted around the place and it was so, so hilarious.

'Oh no!' I said. I looked behind me and there was a platoon of zombies! I screamed!

Finlay Macleod (8)
Bridge Of Allan Primary School, Stirling

My Egypt Summer Holiday

I was going past a pyramid when suddenly a mummy came out of it. It was slathering at the mouth and its hands and arms were like a zombie's. It was chasing me and I hid behind a rock. Then it saw me and it chased me into the pyramid. The pyramid was giant. Then I went into a tunnel and then there was a dead end. The mummy was getting closer to me but I did a backflip into a back handspring over it and I escaped.

Ellie Bruce (7)
Bridge Of Allan Primary School, Stirling

Blood

I went through the desert to a pyramid and a mummy came out. It started to follow me. It was pink and sparkly. After that she chased me to the River Nile and I swam through it. I was so scared. I ran but the mummy kept following me. Monkeys were swinging from the trees and pulled me up before the mummy could catch me!
The mummy was furious. She climbed up the tree to catch me. Eventually, I chopped the mummy's head off and cut the rest of the body up and put it in the dungeon.

Sophi Donaldson (7)
Bridge Of Allan Primary School, Stirling

The Mummy Chasing Me!

When I was walking past a pyramid with Mum and Dad, suddenly a mummy came out. Next, the mummy was chasing us into a pyramid. Then we came across a trap. Then Mum stepped on a bad stone and then the mummy got his head chopped off by a sword. Next my mum fainted and it was very, very hard to pick her up. Eventually, we went to the River Nile and we saw five crocodiles. After a while the crocodiles let us have a ride on them! At last we went home because Mum and Dad were scared.

Robyn Macaskill (7)
Bridge Of Allan Primary School, Stirling

Isis' Catastrophe With Khufu

Isis was watching the parade when she got lost. She wandered around until she came to the Giza Pyramid. Then something came out of the shadows... a mummy!
She started running. There was only one place to go: the Nile. She was almost there when she saw that the mummy was chasing her. She jumped. Isis swam hard, however Khufu's mummy caught her. Khufu dragged Isis to the palace and chucked her in the window, into Ptolemy and Cleopatra's bedroom.
Cleopatra's eyes snapped open and she screamed, 'You will be fed to the crocodiles.' She was.

Morven Brolly (7)
Bridge Of Allan Primary School, Stirling

The Scientist's Adventure

First they went to the time machine and they got to ancient Egypt.
Then the scientist went to the pyramid and discovered more
about the Sphinx.
After that the mummy came out and the mummy was
serving Tutankhamun. The mummy was small and scary. And the
mummy was white.
Then the mummy led them into the pyramid and they killed
Tutankhamun.
At the end they went back home and they brought the mummy
back home with them. When it was in the laboratory it came back
to life!
'Oh no!' said the assistant.
Then it killed him!

Matilde Ferreira Andrade (7)
Bridge Of Allan Primary School, Stirling

Mummy Attack!

I went into a time machine and ended up in Egypt. Then a fierce
mummy came out of a pyramid. After that I ran away and I ended
up at the Nile. I saw a potion and I turned into a crocodile, then
swam across the Nile and found a crossbow. I shot the mummy.
After a while I turned back into a human. In the end I unwrapped
the mummy and killed it. I killed it by chopping its head off and
stamping on it and putting the head in the Nile River and it died.

Joel Notman (8)
Bridge Of Allan Primary School, Stirling

The Horrible Mummy

I was walking past a humungous pyramid in Egypt. It was so hot my feet were burning! A mummy dripping with blood chased me into the pyramid. I didn't know where to go.

I stood on a stone and arrows shot out of the wall. The arrows shot down the corridor at me. They scuffed my ear. It was a tight squeeze. Spikes fell from the sky. I got bandages.

The walls closed. I saw the gold... I sprinted! I got away. The mummy died. It was disgusting, horrible and gruesome.

Bertie Wood (8)
Bridge Of Allan Primary School, Stirling

Likely Tales

Knock! It was Crazy Columbus again. 'What this time?' I asked.
'Another brilliant discovery. The world is round,' the loony told me.
'Yes, and pigs can fly?' I replied.
'Come on Peter Activlet, when have I ever lied to you? Give me an example,' challenged Columbus.
'The so-called 'New World',' I said.
'I've never been so insulted,' he cried.
He stormed off, so outraged I laughed. I wanted to throw a party. I'd play music loud enough to wake my dead Uncle Charles.
Honestly, next thing Crazy Columbus will be telling me is that dogs descended from wolves.

Zoe Carruth (9)
Bridge Of Weir Primary School, Bridge Of Weir

Trapped!

I followed the tourists into the Great Pyramid of Giza, greatly relieved to be out of the boiling Egyptian sun. The tourists marvelled as the tour leader led us towards King Khufu's sarcophagus in a huge, dark room. The tourist group moved on while I went to investigate a pile of gold. I walked towards the sarcophagus but tripped and fell onto it. The lid slipped off and revealed a scroll covered in hieroglyphics. I could see it was very important. I started towards the entrance but as I reached it, it closed. I was trapped!

Zander Tough (9)
Cleish Primary School, Kinross

The Pyramid Asher Built

Asher woke up and felt the roasting heat as a guard came up to his room. The guard growled at him to finish the pyramid, or he would be staying for a year and be whipped. So he went to make the pyramid. He was angry. He had to get up at night to build because a member of the pharaoh's family had died. It was hard work. When he finished he ached, but at least he would get a good reward. The pharaoh made him the most important builder in Egypt as he had worked all alone.

Keilan Callender (8)
Cleish Primary School, Kinross

The Evolution Of Dinos

Tithon T-rex looked around. Chewing a tree was Donus Diplodocus. Over by the river was Rolock Raptor and of course Solo Spinosaurus was starting a fight with Tinon, Tithon's brother. Peering closer, Tithon saw an eagle in-between them. Sneakily, he headed to the fighting dinos and snatched the eagle from under them. Suddenly, something bad happened. Charging down from the hill came humans. They killed every dino that they saw! Tithon didn't run, he started fighting them. Then he realised why they had been running... there was an asteroid coming! He closed his eyes and waited for impact.

Amalie Brown (10)
Cleish Primary School, Kinross

The Major Oak

Robin ran through the forest. He was trying to escape from the sheriff. He had stolen some food from him to give to the poor. Robin could hear the sheriff catching up on his horse and he needed to hide. Suddenly, he spotted a hole in a big oak tree, so he jumped in and hid. The sheriff rode past and didn't catch Robin. 'This is a great hiding spot,' said Robin, 'I will use this from now on!'

Ben Conn (9)
Cleish Primary School, Kinross

The Mummified Pharaoh

I woke up on an early morning. My son came in and told me that the almighty King Tut had fallen in war. I started crying because I was also told I had to mummify the dead body. I screamed in horror. I was given the body and told to take all the internal organs out. I poured salt and natron on the body and left it for forty days.
Afterwards, I wrapped the body with bandages. Once it was done a funeral was held and the body was placed into the Great Pyramid. Everyone was sad.

Archie Somerville (8)
Cleish Primary School, Kinross

Jason And The Argonauts

I woke up and I was in a room in the Colosseum with my friend Jason. I then woke Jason up. I drew my sword and Jason took out his spear. Romans filed into the room, they asked us lots of questions and we answered them carefully. Finally they pushed us out of the room, through the opposite door, into Rome. We ran to where the Argo was moored. Jason shouted to Atalanta, one of his friends on the Argo. She got the ship ready. Eventually, we sailed away to find the 'Golden Fleece'.

Niamh Chumley (9)
Cleish Primary School, Kinross

Building Calamity

As he placed the last brick on the wall, Augustus sighed with relief. He had finished! But then there was the sound of sliding bricks. The house toppled to the floor. 'Nooo!' Augustus felt like crying. *What's the Emperor going to say?* he thought. Just then in walked the Emperor. 'I'm so sorry. I just...' stuttered Augustus, but the Emperor cut him off.

'I don't care, you're banished anyway!'

The Emperor had only banished Augustus because the house he was building was his and now he had nowhere to live.

From that day on, Augustus never built a house again.

Charlotte Jeffrey (9)
Cleish Primary School, Kinross

The Messy Room

So, my mum told me to tidy my room, so I did. It took me two hours but I did it at last. So I went to watch TV. Suddenly it was messy again. So, as before, I tidied it up. This went on and on. It took longer every time but in time I did it and got pocket money. I bought stuff. My sisters didn't help so they didn't get any money. I did. I made my bed and brushed my teeth and watched a movie. Then I went to sleep. In the morning it happened again!

Mackenzie Lisle (11)
Deanston Primary School, Deanston

The Lonely Private

I write this letter to you because it may be my last. We are in the Somme. I have never seen so many fall in such short time. We have barely pushed the Germans back and we have been fighting for months. They call it progress. How I miss the pleasure of a hot bath, a decent meal on my plate, even fresh air and not being shot at every day. My friend, Jimmy, keeps a smile on my face. Can't wait to meet my new daughter. Call her Poppy, after the flower that grows here. Miss you all. Bobby.

Max Clark
Deanston Primary School, Deanston

Jim And The Time Machine

There was once a boy called Jim and he was eleven years old. One night, that all changed for Jim. His friend put him in a time machine whilst sleeping and he went back into 1916 from 1922. Jim was five and he met his grandad. Jim was a five-year-old boy on the outside but inside he was still an 11-year-old. His grandad didn't know Jim, but Jim knew him.
The next day, Jim followed his grandad but his grandad ignored him. Jim awoke. 'Was this a dream or not?' he asked himself.

Lewis Clements (11)
Deanston Primary School, Deanston

The Princess Vs The Robber

One day, when her family were away visiting another King and Queen, Princess Grace spotted a robber from the Emerald Palace lookout. She knew he would try to steal the jewels so Grace ran to get boulders and hot water to scare him away. She threw the boulders and tipped the buckets of water over the robber but he still kept trying to get the jewels. She found a huge stick and knocked him down into the moat. The robber got out the water and ran away because he knew he would never get the jewels. What a brave Princess!

Skye MacDonald (8)
Deanston Primary School, Deanston

The Girl In Egypt

One hot day a girl called Sally went to talk to the emperor Stewart. Sally said, 'I heard a strange noise from the pyramid.' Stewart said, 'Oh, it's probably the bats and rats, so go away little peasant.'
Sally stormed off down the stairs then suddenly she heard it again. This time it sounded like it was coming closer. *Bang!* The door opened then out came a mummy. Sally shouted, 'Paint your faces red!'
Everyone did, including the emperor. Then the mummy dropped down and everyone cheered. 'Sally the Saviour!'

Hannah Lyons (10)
Deanston Primary School, Deanston

David's Worst Night

David was ten years old when the bombs fell from the sky. He was scared, the enemy was bombing the nearby shipyards. David was watching from his house. The dark night sky was now red with fire. There was smoke everywhere. He could hear explosions and sirens; the sound was terrifying. He hoped the enemy would run out of bombs and it would be over soon. His mum told him to come away from the window, it was time to go to the bomb shelter. His mum said the shelter would keep them safe but David didn't feel safe.

Scott Stewart (10)
Deanston Primary School, Deanston

The Magic Stopwatch

Best friends, Lucy and Sophie, decided to take a shortcut through the woods. Lucy stumbled down a hill and she found a half buried stopwatch. She picked it up and clicked the button, transporting herself to a warzone. She got such a fright from all the bombs, sirens and gunfire that she pushed the button and dropped the stopwatch, transporting herself back to 2016.
Lucy heard Sophie call her to see where she was. Lucy responded, 'Did you see those bombs go off?'
Sophie replied, 'Did you hit your head? I'll take you to Mum's!'

Isabella Marshall (10)
Deanston Primary School, Deanston

The Lost Spider Island Treasure

Pirate Captain Kira and her crew were looking for treasure. They needed to find Spider Island. They had been looking for three years with no luck. Captain Kira was close to giving up when one night she noticed a bright red light in the sea. She ordered her crew to sail towards it. As they got closer, she saw huge, dark rocks shaped like a spider. Finally, they had found it! On the island they began to dig where the map showed. After a while they found a golden chest full of beautiful diamonds. The pirates celebrated all night.

Rebecca Stewart (7)
Deanston Primary School, Deanston

The Truly Sad Day!

One morning, Mary Queen of Scots was saying goodbye to Lord Darnley as she was going to a wedding. A few minutes into the wedding, a loud bang shook the town. Mary could see a fire coming from Kirk O'Field, where Darnley was staying!
By the time Mary got back there were ashes on the ground and sticks scattered everywhere!
In the garden, Mary could see Lord Darnley and his servant on the ground. They had not died from the explosion but strangled afterwards, it was truly a sad day!

Bonnie Harzmeyer (10)
Dunlop Primary School, Kilmarnock

I Was In The Past

I was in the past, that was obvious. A medieval castle loomed before me. I had to go in. The castle grounds looked cold and grey. Something nagged at the back of my head but I just couldn't remember what. It was almost impossible to get in. There were loads of guards, the dungeons would be quieter. I was right. They were almost empty. Suddenly, a guard marched from the shadows and unlocked one of the cells. To my surprise an old lady hobbled out and followed the guard into a side room where she knelt down and waited. *Chop!*

Grace Gillan (10)
Dunlop Primary School, Kilmarnock

Goners

'Land ho!' cried the Chief. Britain just came into sight.

'Great, Vikings have been wanting to attack Britain for years,' whispered Willow. Willow wasn't meant to be on the ship, she was a stowaway. Willow hadn't come alone; she came with her white rat, Ratty. Just then the ship stopped. They had arrived. Everyone ran off the ship and started attacking. 'Let's go,' said Willow. They ran off the ship and hid. They watched for a bit but soon fell asleep.

They woke up hours later. The ship had left. They were goners.

Estelle Murray (10)
Dunlop Primary School, Kilmarnock

Hello, I'm A Rat!

'Run, run, run,' squeaked Toby. Toby is a rat. If you haven't already guessed, he carries the plague.

'I'm puffed,' huffed Ben. Ben also carries the plague.

'Duck!' yelled Toby.

'I never knew humans used ducks to catch rats,' said Ben.

'No, duck under the dog's legs,' yelped Toby.

'Woah!' cried Ben, as he slid on his fat tummy.

'Wheee!' squeaked Toby, escaping the dog.

'Ooh, cheese! Yummy!' mumbled Ben.

'Enough eating, you greedy pig,' groaned Toby.

They ran into a house where a baby sat but they left, not giving the baby the plague.

Morven Pennington (10)
Dunlop Primary School, Kilmarnock

A Strange Encounter

I could see a glimpse of the sun piercing through the trees. I walked further and then came out onto grasslands. I could see two men, wearing not clothes, but plants. I assumed they were Aborigines. I started to run towards them. I drew suddenly to a halt. One said, 'Who are you and why are you here?'
'I don't know,' I replied. I started to walk a bit further but could hear footsteps behind me. I turned around and the Aborigines started to run towards me. I came to the edge of a cliff. I jumped...

Grace Brogan (10)
Dunlop Primary School, Kilmarnock

The Death Of Mary

The year was 1587, and Mary Queen of Scots was going to die. The cell had holes for the inmates to claw at her and when she was taken she fell multiple times. 'Get up you!' the executioner said in his deep voice.
'Come on!' a crowd shouted across the hall.
When they got to the block, the crowd were cheering for her death. 'Get on! Just die!'
'Head in the block,' the executioner said.
The crowd shouted, 'Three, two, one!'
Her head rolled.

Scott McBride (10)
Dunlop Primary School, Kilmarnock

Fight, Fight, Fight

The island was right in front of my eyes. It appeared to be dark, soggy and gloomy. Then we came to the shore, ready for a deadly attack. Everyone clambered off the wet, soggy boat and bellowed, 'Charge!' I knew the battle would be finished in a few minutes but I still might die. Then I saw someone in my clan fighting someone else. I helped him take down the opponent. Finally, we won! We had won once again!

Rob Miller (11)
Dunlop Primary School, Kilmarnock

Darnley's Death!

I ran through the gloomy alleyway, past the park, turned past the apple orchard and into the old tavern to see Mary Queen of Scots, the best Queen of Scots! 'How could you get married to Lord Darnley? He's a drunken fool!'
'Erm, who cares?' Mary said, nervously. 'Anyway, can you stay with Darnley at Kirk O'Field?' Mary asked.
'Yes,' I answered.
So off I set to Kirk O'Field. We got there at noon but it didn't take long for someone to try to kill us with explosives! We got out but the murderer choked Darnley and said, 'You're next!'

Reece Denham (10)
Dunlop Primary School, Kilmarnock

The King-Size Mistake!

I knew I was in more trouble than before. I noticed a strange, half-finished sculpture that looked like a man in his teens. Behind the sculpture stood a huge palace that gleamed in the sunlight. I walked into the palace because something important was happening. As I walked up through the entrance, I tripped up over a rock and fell. I picked myself up with the rock in my hand. A guard said, 'The king will be stabbed in one minute.' I panicked and threw the rock at the king instead of the executioner.

Jack Morris (10)
Dunlop Primary School, Kilmarnock

The Magic Button

One morning I browsed the Internet and saw a green glowing button and I pressed it. I appeared in a castle. There were large walls peering over me. There were crowds of people and I saw a man dragging a lady to a block, where a tall man was standing beside the block. I attempted to save her but I failed and I teleported to my bed.

Struan Thomson (11)
Dunlop Primary School, Kilmarnock

Press Me!

I went upstairs to the computer and went on YouTube. I saw a button that said: 'Press Me'. I did. Before I knew it, my bare feet were sinking into hot sand and sweat dripped down my head. 'Ouch!' I shouted. 'My feet.' I must have shouted too loudly, because mummies were now chasing me. I stopped. I couldn't run anymore. My feet were on fire. I looked down. I was on a tile with no sand. *Bing, bang, bong.* I was home!

Nina Porter (10)
Dunlop Primary School, Kilmarnock

Mary's Death

Mary was a queen with a tragic life. I shall tell you about her death...
I was there. Mary was sweet and kind and had no reason to die. I cried my eyes out when the third chop came down. I hoped this was a dream. It wasn't. It was real, deadly real.

Millie Woods (10)
Dunlop Primary School, Kilmarnock

Goodbye Mary

I looked all around and saw the shadow of a big castle. I looked up and saw a humongous castle about fifteen metres high. I walked into the castle anxiously, and walked up the huge, broken stairs. As I went up, the stairs let out a squeak. When I got to the top I saw a woman. She looked a lot like Mary Queen of Scots from a book. She was hobbling up the stairs and looked in a lot of pain. She put her head in the head block. She was praying. Then Elizabeth said, 'Chop off her head!'

Amy Mitchell (11)
Dunlop Primary School, Kilmarnock

Epic Egyptians

Once, on a hot, boiling day, I opened the door, grabbing a rake. The sand whistled and a scorpion shot along the sand dunes. I looked up at the great sandstone pyramid. I stared at the scorpion and smiled. I raked the ground for hours, staring at the sparkling tip of the pyramid. Suddenly, a tall, pale figure with bulging green eyes came up behind me and snapped, 'Go to the pharaoh in the pyramid.'
In the pyramid, I saw two figures grinning. The pharaoh stood up and said, 'You will be pharaoh!' I gulped and stumbled back.

Callum Pennington (9)
Dunlop Primary School, Kilmarnock

Mary Loses Her Head

It was a lovely day in Scotland. Skipping through the forest, I suddenly came to a very tall castle. The castle's doors were almost the size of a giraffe and above them was a sign that said: 'Fotheringhay Castle'. I walked in and saw a lady with her head on a guillotine! I walked up to see who she was. It was Mary Queen of Scots. Then a guard pulled me up and put my head on the guillotine too! One, two, three. *Chop!*

Abbie Curran (10)
Dunlop Primary School, Kilmarnock

The School Trip!

'Right children, come on,' shouted Miss Reid.
We were on a school trip at an Egyptian museum. I walked in and saw a strange box in the corner. I took one step towards the box and *whoosh*, I was in it!
'Could you pass me the hook, Doctor Styles?' asked the figure. There was a large hook being passed between two men. The hook was getting put in a dead man's ear, removing his brain!
'Right, your turn!' he said to me!

Sophie Blackmore (10)
Dunlop Primary School, Kilmarnock

Bat Saves His Family

Bat woke up and his family was gone. He first went into the tombs. He found a coffin and a mummy called Kelly. 'Who are you?' asked Bat.

'I'm Kelly.'

'Have you seen my family?' cried Bat.

'No, but I'll help you.'

'Thank you.'

So they set off! 'Argh!' a loud voice screamed. Bat thought that was his mum. Suddenly they came across a maze. Bat had a brilliant idea. He flew up and guided Kelly through the maze.

'I can fly over and let them out.' So Bat flew over and let his family out. 'You're okay, you two.'

Domhnall Douglas

Eoligarry Primary School, Isle Of Barra

World War II: Searching For Survivors

Danny and John couldn't believe they'd survived the horrific bombing. Danny whispered, 'We have to search for survivors.' 'OK,' replied John.

They searched throughout houses in Munich. Finally, they heard screaming.

'That has to be a survivor,' said John.

'Yes,' cried Danny.

They dashed over to the survivor but the person was tangled up in rope and rubbish. John and Danny tried to untangle the person, but it was no use. They ended up finding a knife. John tried cutting off the rope and Danny was holding the person still. Finally they cut the rope so the person was free!

Darren MacNeil (9)
Eoligarry Primary School, Isle Of Barra

The Time Adventures

I was swimming in the sea and me and my crew saw a jungle. Me and Tim found a boat then we went for a run in the jungle. It was fun. There was an animal in the bushes but it was Jake, a jungle girl. She was scared because nobody loved her or went there. 'It is very boring here,' she whispered. I met her and we went out on the boat Tim found. We rowed away on the boat and had a great time.

Sophie Mitchell (8)
Hallglen Primary School, Falkirk

Raptors Vs Cavemen

Bug was wandering around collecting wood. He built a spear. He collected wood for his house then Bug started hunting lizards. He also discovered fire and made flame torches.
Later on, he started hunting dinosaurs! His first caveman friend was Bobby and his first dinosaur kill was a diplodocus.
One day they met three raptors! After a day, they'd killed two. 'Yay!' they shouted. Then raptors ate Bobby! Bug was angry. He killed the raptor viciously. Sadly, victory did not last. A pterosaur swooped away with him and threw him into an active volcano. No, seriously, it was active.

Douglas Stephen (8)
Hallglen Primary School, Falkirk

The Magical Adventure

A long time ago a girl named Jade saw her parents die in a fire. She still had her best friend.

Two days after her parents died, dinosaurs attacked the village. Ozzy and Jade were the only people left, so Jade and Ozzy went to the gun shop to kill the dinosaur.

When they were killing, there were more dinosaurs from a cave. These dinosaurs were friendly, they bought them candy from the shop, bought them toys, books, even scooters. They even treated them like their own children.

Abby Rose Honeyman (8)
Hallglen Primary School, Falkirk

Fighting For France

'Off to France we go,' Taylor said.

'Let's go help France,' said Kevin and Frank.

'Stay focused,' said Sam, staying calm.

'We are landing now,' said the pilot over the radio.

When the crew was dropped off they knew how serious it was, so they stayed focused. They went out and fought. Then Kevin became injured so the crew had to lift him up and take him to the plane. They went with Kevin and went back once they knew Kevin was okay.

While going back, all that they could think of was their families.

Fraser Christie (11)
Hallglen Primary School, Falkirk

The Lost Princess Cleopatra

On a sunny day the daughter of the queen was born, Princess Cleopatra. That night, a wicked old lady broke into the castle and took her. Cleopatra cried and cried until suddenly, a big bang went off. It was the guards bashing through the wooden door. 'Go away,' shouted the lady. The guards followed her down to the river and got the baby. When they got back, the king and queen had a big celebration and the whole village was invited. There were balloons, a buffet and a big, fun chariot race. They got the baby and lived happily ever after.

Ashleigh Elizabeth Wilson (11)
Hallglen Primary School, Falkirk

Cavemen And Romans Fight

There were four cavemen. They were in the Cave of Lights. One day, the Romans came and all four cavemen died. The Romans had a party all day long. They were very happy. Some other cavemen came home. When they got home, the Romans were there. They had a fight, it took all day long and the next day they fought again. It took two more days but the Romans died. The Roman empire sent more out. When the caveman went out of the cave, they ran back in away from the Romans. The cavemen died.

Kelsie Middleton (8)
Hallglen Primary School, Falkirk

Jack's World War II Story

Me and Bob the king both have minions and my minions fight Bob's minions. We were in a forest, it was raining. Oh no, it was night. 'Everybody, get your flashlight and put it on your gun.' Oh no, one of my minions died.

'Kill them,' I said.

'Kill them, you fools,' Bob said.

All of our minions died. Then it was time for me and Bob to fight each other.

I won. 'Yay!' Oh no, there were two of his minions. I shot them. 'Well, it looks like I win. Hahaha, you're dead!'

Jack Aitchison (8)
Hallglen Primary School, Falkirk

A Girl And A Dinosaur

Once upon a time there was a girl named Bell. She had a sister but she never knew her. Her sister's name was Alyse. Bell was walking home with her dad and then a girl came up to her and said, 'I am your sister and my name is Alyse.'

Then Bell said, 'This is really weird, I don't have any sisters.' Then she saw a dinosaur. Then Bell said to her dad, 'I want to go home, this is getting weird.' Then she said, 'Actually, can we be friends?'

They all became friends.

Wiktoria Kaleta (8)
Hallglen Primary School, Falkirk

Forest Dinosaur

One day, deep in a forest, there were two bad dinosaurs called Alfie and Coco. They always went round with axes killing people but something strange happened: they couldn't kill one person. His name was Gary Dotter. They killed his mum and dad but they couldn't kill Gary. After they killed someone, they would take them to their base which was a big, dark cave called The Bad Cave. That's where they put all their dead bodies. There was one more person to kill. Gary Dotter never got killed, he killed them then he ruled the world.

Kyle Cringean (9)
Hallglen Primary School, Falkirk

The Dinosaur Dance-Off

One day two dinosaurs came to eat two cavemen called Ugga and Bobby. The two cavemen were making cocoa shakes. They looked out the window and saw two dinosaurs. They offered the cocoa shakes to them so the dinosaurs would not eat them. The dinosaurs said, 'We will not eat you, but only if we have a dance-off.'
It was a tie, the dinosaurs had two and the cavemen had two. Then the Ice Age came. The dinosaurs died and the cavemen won. They celebrated with cocoa shakes. Mmm, tasty.

Mia Ann Tracey (8)
Hallglen Primary School, Falkirk

35

The Haunted House

This is about a little girl. The girl was coming home from school into a haunted house. Two minutes later, she got dragged into the house. She was screaming, shouting, kicking, punching and biting. Then her dog smelled the blood, so it went up to the house but then ran away. It was so scared it was shivering. The wee girl was never seen again.

Mckenzie Craig (8)
Hallglen Primary School, Falkirk

The Great Dave

Once upon a time there were two cavemen, one was a father and the other was a son. When they were walking, a T-rex came up to them and the father got eaten by the T-rex. The son, called Dave, ran into his cave and went as deep as he could go.
Fifty years later, he grew up and he was undefeatable. He killed the T-rex that'd eaten his father. He saved villages from dinosaurs.
One day, the Roman army came up to him and said, 'We will fight you, Dave.' Dave defeated the army with victory.

Arran Richardson (8)
Hallglen Primary School, Falkirk

Caveman Life

Once there lived two cavemen called Bug and Bobby. Bug was the son, Bobby was the dad. They were scared of the dark but they went for a walk in the dark. Suddenly, they heard a noise coming from behind. *Splat!* Bobby was gone forever and Bug was so upset. He survived, although he got bitten on the leg, he'd have a scar for the rest of his long life. He limped home. Bug used to have a club but now he had a diamond sword. He could take care of himself now.

Emma-Louise Ferrier (8)
Hallglen Primary School, Falkirk

The Bob Apocalypse

Long ago there was a dinosaur and a caveman who mixed their blood together and made the Bob-virus. Everyone was infected. Only one person could stop it, Stan! Stan was sitting in his house when an infected boy came in. His son! He went into his top-secret lab and created a cure. He put it in his son's mouth. 'Argh!' he screamed. Stan asked everybody he knew who wasn't eliminated to punch him into the black hole. He flew into the void, destroyed the space time continuum and destroyed himself with it, creating a fake Earth.

Lucas Beck (9)
Hallglen Primary School, Falkirk

When Thor's Day Went Wrong

Once upon a time, on Thorsday, Thor was enjoying his special day. It started going wrong because an evil Viking had to ruin the fun. Thor couldn't stand it so cancelled Thorsday and took the evil Viking to Odin, Freya and Loki. Freya said, 'Why are you ruining Thorsday?'
'Well, I want to find someone for my master, but I can't find them and my master said after you catch them, ruin Thorsday, so I did.' Thor thought he should put Thorsday on again and so he did. Everyone was invited.

Ella Gibson (7)
Hallglen Primary School, Falkirk

Mummies Are Good [Not]

Mummies are good, everyone says. That's what Papa and I thought anyway. We had won a midnight trip to the museum. We were walking along the poorly lit corridor in the Egyptian section. We were looking at all the exhibits when we heard footsteps padding behind us. We looked round and there was a tall figure, all covered in bandages. It was a 'real' mummy. I screamed, Papa screamed like a big girl and we started to run. We got outside the museum and I said to Papa, 'Mummy wasn't looking too good was she?' He laughed.

Nicole Claire Padkin (8)
Hallglen Primary School, Falkirk

Back In Time For Homework

'Emma,' said Mrs Count, Emma's teacher, 'I heard you were having trouble with your history homework. How about you go see Mr Clock?'

'OK.'

'Hello,' said Mr Clock. He was a short man with white hair. 'I have a good way to help. Go into this machine.'

'How did we get to the Victorian times? Wow, there is Queen Victoria. Now I know what project I am going to do.'

'How did it go with Queen Victoria?'

'Good, thank you.'

'Emma?'

'Yes?'

'Could you not tell anyone about my time machine?'

'Bye, Mr Clock.'

'Bye, Emma. I will miss you.'

Hope Griffin (11)
Hallglen Primary School, Falkirk

The Fight

Once there was a princess called Alissa and she had to make a decision, a very hard decision. Over boys. I know, gross right? But it had to happen. So the fight began. You'd be surprised how many people showed up: 120. Amazing, ain't it? OK, the fight started. The two people who were fighting were called Jaden the Poor Man and Lewis the Rich Man. OK, now it was starting. Oh no, Rich Man Lewis was on the floor. Wow, it looked like Poor Man Jaden was the winner. The princess was really glad.

Regan Grierson (8)
Hallglen Primary School, Falkirk

Food War

'OK brother, let's fight for action and fight the queen. Let's go. I found the castle. Let's rule the world and help people to live.'
'Hello? What are you doing in here? Are you trying to make an announcement? Are you or not? Tell me the truth?'
'We are here to see you.'
'Oh really? Sorry then.'
'That's OK.'
'Boys, I am going to sleep now. Goodbye.'
'Bye,' said the boys.
12.30 at night. 'Let's go break in and rule the world.'
'OK.'
'3, 2, 1, go!'
'She is dead!'
'Yes, let's eat and have so much fun and enjoyment.'

Eilidh Thomson (8)
Hallglen Primary School, Falkirk

John The Dinosaur And The Caveman

One day there was a dinosaur who killed everyone and there was a man who tried to protect everyone and to kill the dinosaur. Once, an earthquake almost killed everyone. Some stayed alive and weren't killed by it. Then a tornado happened and all the trees disappeared because the tornado took all the trees away. John and Nate saw each other and Nate got his sword out, his diamond sword, and went for John who was too busy killing. Nate turned his back. Dead!

Nathan Walker (8)
Hallglen Primary School, Falkirk

The Roman Army

My story is going to be about a family going to see the Roman film and the babies were scared of the film. They ate popcorn and had juice. It was nice and the mum and dad had a cup of coffee. The babies had some milk. The Romans were beginning to fight each other. They had swords and guns. They began to shoot and cut people up. Then a big dinosaur came in and ran away. He was laughing at the Romans. The Roman army got really big then they lived happily ever after.

Ruby McNamee (8)
Hallglen Primary School, Falkirk

Jev's Longhouse

Jev was working on his longhouse. He ran out of wood. 'Oh no!' he sighed. 'I think we'll have to go get more wood,' he said to his wolf. So he went on the longship. They were on the longship for days. They were hungry. The waves got bigger and bigger. Jev was scared. Lightning struck and thunder roared in the clouds. *Crack!* The ship hit rocks. The ship sank. Jev and his wolf swam to land. He woke up and there was wood everywhere. He was in Norway. He decided to stay and build a longhouse!

Connor Jackson (10)
Hamnavoe Primary School, Shetland

The Beheading

I was walking in my castle when one of my guards came running towards me. He said, 'New people!' I was thrilled to hear such good news. A moment later she was standing before me, a beautiful woman. I fell in love with her. I decided to marry her: Anne. I beheaded my second wife to marry Anne because she was the one for me. Soon me and Anne were outside at the beheading stage. Later, my executionist came and executed Catherine Howard, my second wife. Me and Anne watched Catherine be beheaded. Me and Anne lived happily together...

Elise Rendall (9)
Hamnavoe Primary School, Shetland

Clara And Rock Stone Age People

Today, outside, whilst I was walking and hunting for food, I met this strong caveman called Rock. We decided to get married today. After the marriage we decided to have a child.
Two years later when Issam (our son) was one, we were invaded by the slim, slick, sabre-toothed tiger. We ran and ran for our lives, well Issam was carried. It caught up with me. I tried to go faster but said to Rock, 'Take Issam.' He did. He came to me and took Issam. Suddenly Blade, the sabre-toothed tiger, dragged me away. Gladly Issam's alive.

Caitlin Kok (9)
Hamnavoe Primary School, Shetland

The Trojan Whippet

'I've got a brilliant idea,' Servus shouted, 'we shall make a wooden whippet!' After Servus had made the wooden whippet he knocked on the door of the city. The soldiers came out and thought the whippet was a present from the gods. That night when everyone was sleeping the Trojan army came out and the guards all woke up. But it was too late. All the guards were slaughtered. Most of them were dead and the rest had been badly injured. When all the guards were dead Servus had saved the king. The Trojans had won.

Logan Tait (10)
Hamnavoe Primary School, Shetland

The World War Adventure

I was in my muddy trench, setting up my machine guns. I heard a loud bang to tell me and my army men the battle had started. The Germans charged for us as fast as a spotty cheetah running. Some of my army men got killed or wounded. I was on my own apart from one last army man alive. Five minutes later he got killed so I was on my own! I fired my gun. I was out of ammo. Then, all of a sudden, a fighter jet came and killed all the Germans. We won the world war.

Lewis Drever
Hamnavoe Primary School, Shetland

The Gruesome Fight

Thernasaurus was walking on the beach and God spawned a chareanadonasaurus then in a flash the thernasaurus sprinted two miles into the jungle. They met in the desert. Therna had really sharp claws so he scratched Chareana down her neck. Blood ran down her neck. Chareana took a chomp out of Therna's rear, pulling out lots of feathers. In the distance they saw a big dinosaur approaching, it was a spinosaurus. Spinosaurus charged! With his crocodile jaw he broke the neck of Thernasaurus, who lay dying on the ground. Spinosaurus sliced and chomped at Charneana who collapsed and died.

Keegan Brown (10)
Hamnavoe Primary School, Shetland

World War I

We were stuck in our trench. A bullet came through the air. I'd ducked in the nick of time. I sniped a guy in the face and blood came flying out. Somebody named James shot somebody in the arm. I walked out in the battlefield and shouted, 'Let's play football to end the war.' I found a leather ball and played. I scored seven goals, the score was 14-11 to the Brits. We had food and drink with our German friends. Then a flare went up and it was time to return to battle again.

Ellis Young (9)
Hamnavoe Primary School, Shetland

The Pirate

A girl pirate sets off on an epic adventure to find her own land. She has taken tons of food on her pirate ship as well as her bird. She goes from Kenmore to Dundee, down the Tay river. She has taken her sword. She swims to the first island. She sees it is full of gold and she meets a lion. She names her island Fairy Dust Island. She discovers that other people live there too. They were her best mate and her old crew, it was a dream come true. 'I can't believe it! I will stay here.'

India Ross (9)
Kenmore Primary School, Aberfeldy

Pirate Fort

There was an island in the Caribbean called Nassau. The most fierce captain on the island was Captain Blackbeard because he scared everyone off. He lit his beard so it smoked a lot and he looked like a devil. The English Navy didn't dare to go there. They had a fort on a cliff with very strong cannons to defend the island. Captain Vane tried to get more people for his crew. He and Captain Rackham tried to attack merchant ships to get all their treasures. The Royal Navy chased all the pirates to hang them. Finally they could escape.

Aileen Sporleder (8)
Kenmore Primary School, Aberfeldy

Untitled

One day, long, long ago, there was an ancient tribe of Vikings. There were four of them, they were called Thor, Taichi, Tarben and Tatsuo. They were getting ready for going out to sea. They were just getting ready when something humongous sprung from the bushes. One of the Vikings shouted, 'Dragon! Run!' The dragon was massive and the Vikings all ran. The dragon was a young dragon but it was still very strong. The Vikings grabbed the rest of their stuff and ran to the longship. They jumped onto the boat and set sail.

Murray Weir (8)
Kenmore Primary School, Aberfeldy

Knight And Dragon

The knight lived in his kingdom with his father. One day a fierce warrior came to the village. He came to attack and collected seven girls and seven boys. The young knight asked to go and his father agreed. He set off on an adventure because he wanted to save the children. The knight rode his dragon to the temple and he got tied to a post for three days and nights. He made a noise and suddenly a knife appeared. He cut the rope and he stabbed the wildebeest and the mean, cruel, selfish warrior.

Max England (7)
Kenmore Primary School, Aberfeldy

The Pirates Who Came To Town

One day some pirates showed up for no reason. I asked what their names were but all they said was, 'Ahar, me hearties!' We looked at each other. We were perplexed because we didn't know what they were saying. We Googled it but still didn't understand it because it meant 'hello my friend'. I didn't know, because I didn't know pirate language, that they were looking for our golden coins. We didn't have any. We didn't know what to do as we had given all our coins to the poor people. The pirates left in disgust.

Annie Dott (7)
Kenmore Primary School, Aberfeldy

The Fake Traitor

Adjudicus and Minicus were Roman troop leaders going into battle. Shortly before the battle begun, Adjudicus saw Minicus whispering to the enemy troops. Adjudicus carefully crept up behind Minicus and eavesdropped on their conversation, but didn't say anything in fear of being caught or killed. During the battle Adjudicus spilled his secret to Minicus about listening to what his plan was and violently slit his throat open. After the battle ended Adjudicus asked the one remaining survivor of the enemy team why Minicus was helping their troops. He said they'd threatened to kill Adjudicus if Minicus did not obey them.

Adam Hitchins (9)
Kenmore Primary School, Aberfeldy

The Dragon Slayer

'100 days,' said my cellmate, looking out the barred window. I was trying to pick the lock without the guard seeing me. 'Cameross it's me,' yelled Ezio. 'Tie this rope to the cell door.' The only thing I saw next was blood and fire. 'Wake up!' bellowed Ezio. A deafening scream made me jump up! My cellmate was burning in the fire, he died trying! We fled through the maze. In the centre was a mighty dragon. 'Take this sword, kill the dragon. It's your fight now,' said Ezio. Who will win? Man versus dragon. 'Let's fight!'

Cameron Kimpton (8)
Kenmore Primary School, Aberfeldy

Dun An Sticir

I would not give up my land to anyone! This is how it all started. My stepmother and I were happy and safe. Later on men surrounded the door, looking for me so I swam away. My stepmother betrayed me and I was captured. I was flung into a dungeon. I shouted for my dear life. I was forced to eat salty meat. I tried to dig with my bones but I knew my death would be soon.

Jack MacDonald (8)
Lochmaddy Primary School, Isle Of North Uist

Hugh's Gory Story

In the 16th century Hugh claimed to own land in North Uist. Cousin Donald was enraged by this so became determined to capture Hugh. Hugh and his stepmother scrambled to the safety of Dun an Sticir. Hugh decided to swim to another islet for fear of capture. His stepmother betrayed him. Hugh was captured and thrown into a dungeon in Duntulm Castle in Skye. He was fed salt beef so Hugh used the bones to scrape at the walls. Weak and thirsty, Hugh gave up and sadly perished.

Andrew MacDonald (11)
Lochmaddy Primary School, Isle Of North Uist

Hugh Is Dead

Hugh is going to swim away from his cousin's island because he is terrified of him. Hugh gives up and then he gets taken away to a castle in Skye where he gets shoved into the dungeons. Hugh is eating salted beef and he tries to break free but he dies of the salt from the beef.

Charlie MacDonald (10)
Lochmaddy Primary School, Isle Of North Uist

Dun An Sticir

'It's mine, like it or not!' exclaimed Hugh. Hugh was wary of Donald and took refuge in Dun an Sticir with his stepmother. He knew Donald's men would catch him so he swam to another islet. What Hugh didn't know was that his stepmother would betray him. Hugh was captured by his cousin and was flung into a dungeon. Hugh had to eat salted beef, still on the bone. The bones were strong so he attempted to scrape the walls but day by day he became thirstier. 'I fear I may perish...'

Anna MacDonald (9)
Lochmaddy Primary School, Isle Of North Uist

The Gory Tale Of Dun An Sticir

Over in the Outer Hebrides a man called Hugh owned some land. His cousin, Donald, hated this; he wanted his land back. As they crept to a little island Hugh's stepmother announced, 'I'll see if it's safe.' Hugh trusted her but she betrayed him by telling Donald he had swam away. Donald's men pulled him by the legs, knocked him out and threw him in the dungeon in Duntulm Castle in Skye. They fed him salted beef. Hugh tried to break the walls with the bones. He took one last hit but the bones snapped and so did his heart.

Blair MacKenzie (8)
Lochmaddy Primary School, Isle Of North Uist

Hugh Was Captured

'You will never get your hands on my land, Donald!' screamed Hugh.
'Yes I will, Hugh!' shrieked Donald, the chief of Clan Huistean. Hugh's stepmother betrayed Hugh by telling Donald that he had swum away to an islet for safety from Donald's men. They'd been sent to capture Hugh because Donald wanted Hugh's land all for himself. Hugh was captured and fed salted beef with bones. Hugh tried to scrape the bones on the wall so he could break out of the dungeon but unfortunately he perished before he could escape.

Katie MacAulay (10)
Lochmaddy Primary School, Isle Of North Uist

Dun An Sticir

'This is my land, my land and no one is going to take it away!' Cousin Donald was cross with me and told my stepmother to capture me.

Once Stepmother called me and said, 'Come here right now.' So I did. Later, I saw some people. They grabbed me, took me to a dungeon and shoved me in. They then dumped in some chunks of very salty beef. I used some bones to try and scrape the walls to escape. As days went by I was weak, tired and thirsty and felt like I was going to perish...

Rachel Morrison (11)
Lochmaddy Primary School, Isle Of North Uist

The Runaway

Where am I? Where have I gone? Where have I run to? The battle has started and the English are invading. I find myself in the woods and make myself a small den. Shivering, I creep into the den to stay warm. I get out my food and begin to eat, though I'm scared as I can hear the banging sounds going off in the distance. I want to see more, although I'm scared. My life has been turned upside down by this battle and I can do nothing. I want the battle of Bannockburn to end.

Grace Berry (10)
Longforgan Primary School, Dundee

Tommy Jerky

I've just lost my arm to embedded shrapnel. Seven men killed. I'm marching back to the Somme. As we approached the front the battle hit home. Bodies lay motionless, they'd fallen dead in front of us from the firing stand to the floor. They were advancing rapidly, it was too much. I was running, trying to get away. I had gone past seven trenches before I got back to base. I was met by Corporal May who wasn't happy at all and sent me to the firing squad for cowardice to be shot that day at 1:30pm.

Campbell Thomson (10)
Longforgan Primary School, Dundee

Adam

Hello, I'm Adam, 3rd in line to the throne. Sorry about that, I got carried away. I am a very brave soldier. I saw people slaughtered, trying to save people I didn't even know. I have never been so scared in my life, seeing more of my friends dying. I'll never forget the scenes I saw at Bannockburn. I'm glad we won and hope that I'll never fight in another battle again.

Adam Laing (10)
Longforgan Primary School, Dundee

Untitled

What have I put myself into? WWI! Guns, tanks, I think in my head as I walk into the French warzone. *I hope I don't die!* Just think, *this is for my country.* The guns begin to fire. I freeze. I feel so petrified. Everyone begins to run. I don't know what to do. 'Run!' everyone shouts. I finally get the idea that I have to run. Days pass, so do nights. Running and shooting, killing and running, I'm even feeling sorry for the other side. I hate war.

Ruby Blackmore (11)
Longforgan Primary School, Dundee

The Battle Of Jebadia

I am in Greece, in the ancient arena, waiting for Jebadia and Dactios to start the chariot race. Oh, here they are. Jebadia is on one side and Dactios is on the other. The whistle has gone, they charge at each other. Jebadia dodges Dactios' arrow and charges at Dactios with a sword. They clash swords. Jabadia shoots an arrow at Dactios and hits his horse. Dactios gets off his chariot and shoots Jebadia's horse. It's man versus man. They both have no arrows so it's swords. Jebadia runs at Dactios and throws his sword at Dactios and hits him.

Logan James Roy Soutar (10)
Longforgan Primary School, Dundee

Titanic Adventure

Finally, today is mine and Ross' last day on the ship. I'm actually pretty happy to leave so I can go back home. 'Argh!' The part of the ship we're standing on is breaking apart and falling. We're all tumbling off the ship with cupboards and tables falling off as well. People are drowning and dying. A table just fell on Ross' face. I swam over to see him. Unfortunately, he was dead. I swam as far away from the ship as possible. I found land and thought to myself, *I feel bad for the others but I'm glad I'm alive.*

Orla Stewart (11)
Longforgan Primary School, Dundee

The Captain's Tale

Splash! The old man falls into the water and doesn't resurface. It's freezing on this cramped boat as we leave behind what's left of the Titanic. Hundreds of freezing swimmers plead to be let onboard only be sent to their cold deaths! Soon we will reach our saviours and I fear when we do that it will all be real. All the guilt, for it was me who ignored the warnings, it was me who believed the Titanic was invincible. As we slow I clamber out the wooden boat and everything becomes real.

Caelan Milne (11)
Longforgan Primary School, Dundee

The Crash

He was born February 1873. He built the Titanic. He was an Irish businessman and shipbuilder. Thomas was reportedly last seen by John Stewart, a steward on the ship at 2:10am, ten minutes before the Titanic sank. Thomas was one of my many friends. He was the owner of the Titanic when it sank. It was a dark night and he was just walking with his cigarette in the steward room when the crash hit. He was falling and he died at the bottom of the sea.

Amy Johnston (9)
Longforgan Primary School, Dundee

Guy Fawkes

Guy Fawkes did not like the king and didn't like his decisions so he made a plan and set off to find the king. He was happy about this. He found the king and under the king's room was a cellar. He sneaked in there. He brought bags of gunpowder and loaded them in. Someone found out about Guy Fawkes' plan and told the king. The king told his knights and his knights went down into the cellar and killed him. He didn't have time to set off the gunpowder. This all happened in the Houses of Parliament.

Georgia Thomson (9)
Longforgan Primary School, Dundee

The Caveman Catastrophe!

'My life is miserable,' moaned the caveman, 'I'm never going to get out of here!' The cave was massive and the caveman was lost. He managed to climb. Suddenly he heard a noise. Another lonely caveman walked in. He tried to help him out. *Crash!* The cave started falling. They ran for ages and found a secret slide. They went down it. Out they came. Soon their lives weren't so miserable after all.

Emma Henderson (10)
Longforgan Primary School, Dundee

The Titanic

I woke up and suddenly became aware of a horrible feeling, much, much worse than sea sickness. My mum and dad were standing in front of me. 'Come on,' said Mum.
I got up and obediently followed my parents around the ship. They were running as if their lives depended on it. We raced past many different rooms, up staircases and along corridors. 'What's happening?' I asked my mum.
'Just run!' she answered.
We eventually reached a lifeboat with lots of worried-looking people in it. 'What?' I asked Dad.
'The Titanic is sinking as we speak,' my dad answered.

Callum Bradley (9)
Longforgan Primary School, Dundee

The Tear Shedding Kidnap

I sat at the table. I heard screams. I ran through the door, it was too late. I shouted, 'Mum! Dad!' I heard crying. A man with chains grabbed me. My arms were cut and sore. I couldn't see anything. I heard people talking.
A lady said, 'Where are we going? Where are you taking my children?'
'England, the best country in the world.'
'No, you can't take them there.'
'Yes I can,' said the man.
'No!' was the last thing I heard.

Grace Prest (9)
Longforgan Primary School, Dundee

The Great Escape

There was a gag in my mouth, choking me. Muscular men dragged me, my arms and legs flailing. They took me to the queen's palace and released my gag. The next morning I was awoken early and taken on a tour around the spectacular palace. The rest of my day was dreadful. It was full of being yelled at by the queen and feeling homesick. Weeks went by - the same. A month later, I was preparing for the millennium feast and I dropped the food. I received a huge punishment so I decided to escape. It was too late.

Sahar Jafferbhoy (10)
Longforgan Primary School, Dundee

World War I

It was all quiet and two of the Scottish soldiers were walking through the field, quite happily thinking that everyone had stopped bombing. It turned out the Germans were just getting ready for a big bombing session. Everyone took cover in trenches or wherever they could. No one wanted to die. They wanted to go home and see their families. At the end of the war one of the Scottish soldiers who was walking through the field died, never to see his family again. However the other man was on his way home to surprise his family, hopefully forever.

Niamh McMahon (11)
Longforgan Primary School, Dundee

Cleopatra And The Horrible War

I'm the last of the pharaohs, all the others are dying in this blood-curdling war. I still have my three children... but not my husband, Mark Antony. I can't die in this war, we'll overcome the Greeks. There are still pharaohs endlessly fighting for me. We'll never retreat. My husband heard that I'd died but I hadn't. He was so upset he tried to kill himself but didn't stab himself properly so didn't die. Then he heard that I hadn't died so he got carried to me. Then he did die. I was so upset I did kill myself.

Reuben McCulloch (10)
Longforgan Primary School, Dundee

Captain Edward J Smith

It was a nice night on the ship when suddenly we all heard the alarm going off. It was so shocking to hear the alarm. The lookouts got a warning but they ignored it. Two hours later we started to sink. Captain Smith decided to stay on because he knew he had to get off last. They said we could not get off until all the ladies get off with their children. All you could hear was screaming. We could not believe that two men jumped off nor that the fuel tank fell down. The screaming got louder.

Lucy Stoves (9)
Longforgan Primary School, Dundee

Roman War

I woke up to another Roman war. I thought the Roman Empire was making the wrong choice to fight in this war. I marched outside and got my armour on. 'Get on the boats and win the Latin war!' shouted the emperor. I got on the boat. I was steering the boat and controlling the catapults. The only weapons I had were my sword, bow and a smaller catapult. We finally won the Latin war, the Pyrrhic War and the Punic war. The last war against Barbatus there was black smoke and arrows everywhere. People were drowning. We were defeated...

Owen Smith (10)
Longforgan Primary School, Dundee

Cleopatra

Cleopatra was sitting on her bed crying; all her make-up was getting ruined and her servants were trying to fix it. She was crying because the man she loved had died. To get her mind off it she decided to go on a journey through Egypt. It was long, dangerous and scary. Her servants trailed behind her. Halfway through her journey she saw a cobra. Still in tears and still stressed, she picked up the cobra, strangled it and put it right to her face. It got angry and killed her.

Ailidh Milne (10)
Longforgan Primary School, Dundee

Guy Fawkes

Guy Fawkes was told to be a great brutal and terrifying sight. He did not like the king's ideas so he really wanted to change them and kill him. One night he was going to kill the king with some other people. Somehow someone found out and told the king he was in great danger! They told him to look in his dungeon so he sent guards down to check. He told the king he was right and Guy Fawkes and his plan got found out about. He got executed. So remember, remember, the fifth of November: Firework Night.

Eve Stewart (9)
Longforgan Primary School, Dundee

New Discovery

I've always dreamed of landing on the moon and my training started from 1930, all the way to 2012. I was training with NASA, that stands for National Aeronautic Space Administration. I'll tell you what I did with NASA... I went in lots and I mean lots of simulators. I went to space with Mike Collins and Erving E Aldrin. When I landed on the moon I took a big leap on the moon.

Fraser Johnston (9)
Longforgan Primary School, Dundee

The Magic Pyramid

It was a very hot day and Chaz the mummy was going to the magic pyramid. As he was going he saw Bob, his friend, and they both went to the pyramid. As they walked in Chaz pressed a button and they went through the door. The lights switched off and they went on a huge water slide. It was so slippy. Soon they were at the bottom of the slide. After the slide Bob saw a button. Bob pressed it and there appeared a big pot of gold. They took it!

Abbey Mailley (10)
Longforgan Primary School, Dundee

The Trojans

The time has finally come. It's really hot in here and I am sweating so much. We've been waiting for hours to get moved. We are all cramped in together. 'When do you think we will get pulled in?' asked Acamas.

'Well we've banged on the door enough. Oh, I think we're on the move!' said Odysseus.

As night falls, the soldiers sneak out of the horse with their swords and weapons. 'Do you think the Trojans will find out?' asked Polypoetes in a worried voice.

'Oh no, of course not, it's the middle of the night,' replied Odysseus.

Áine Coad (11)
Loretto Junior School, Musselburgh

Warrior Horse

The stable is cold and screams of the other horses fill the air. As we walk to the field, there is a loud noise. The battle has begun. The ground is muddy so my hooves get stuck. I jump to get my feet free. My rider falls, a strange object is pointed at me. A small metal thing whizzes past, nearly hitting me. I gallop away from it; the noise spooked me. My legs are tired. I feel like I am going to fall, I have been here so long. There are flags waving and cheering, it is over.

Evie McNamara (10)
Loretto Junior School, Musselburgh

Back In Time

We were in a mall, going to the second floor. We pressed button number two. Then, the elevator started shaking and we went really fast towards the ground.

'Argh, this is so scary,' said Josh.

'This is so epic,' I shouted. Then, the door opened. We walked out and we saw nothing.

'Did you hear that?' whispered Josh. We looked up and saw a dinosaur. Then, the dinosaur opened his mouth. Then, I pushed Josh towards the dinosaur. It bit Josh's head off.

Then, I ran into the elevator. 'I hope this takes me back.'

Yassin Shaker (8)
Loretto Junior School, Musselburgh

A Horse Made For Battle

We build a wooden horse to sneak into Troy. The big gates open and the Persians think the massive wooden horse is a present for winning the battle. Everyone getting ready for war is anxious and nervous and hoping everything will go to plan as tension builds in the big horse. The Persians start to pull in the massive wooden horse, not knowing we are inside. We start to creep out as night falls, all ready for battle. Then we attack the city of Troy.

Michael Williams (11)
Loretto Junior School, Musselburgh

History With A Twist

We were climbing up the mountain when the storm hit. George and I were nearly at the summit. We took cover until daybreak. By then we were chilled to the bone. We got up and resumed our climbing. Then we had another problem: our oxygen was dangerously low. On top of that George wasn't dealing well with the altitude. We had to be quick. We reached the summit, just in the nick of time. I felt my knees buckling beneath me but I could just about make it down. Luckily, George and I made it down safely.

Tom Shanks (10)
Loretto Junior School, Musselburgh

The Frozen Land

My family and I settled in Iceland, which is freezing! Not long after that, I got banished from this new land. As I'm a Viking explorer, I set out to the Gunnbjörn Islands. I brought a crew with me, who didn't know what to expect. I also went down to the southern tip of Greenland, where I spent my next two glacial winters. When my banishment was over, I called the new land Greenland (though it was covered in ice!). I encouraged and led settlers there, but most died of starvation or disappeared.

Janica Chan (10)
Loretto Junior School, Musselburgh

HMS Britannic

The Britannic helped those wounded in war but the submarine that protected the Britannic was sunk by a mine. Next voyage, I sailed out the harbour and sailed for two days until a U-boat fired a torpedo at us. We started sinking but the ship still went forward and soon the bow was underwater and the propellers were visible. The ship got slower and chopped up a lifeboat. I saw it then the ship started to capsize. The last thing I saw of the ship was the stern plunge. Thirty-one people died.

Rory Kemp (10)
Loretto Junior School, Musselburgh

A Despicable Plan

Dark and cold it was, as I crept into the cellar. I let out a small sigh of relief as I reached the base of my despicable plan. I beckoned my accomplices to follow. I gestured to the gunpowder barrel. Small smirks spread across our faces. Though the cold was biting, we managed to reach the barrels without being spotted. *5th of November, 1605 - It will go down in history!* thought I. I reached to light the barrel. I was about to achieve my goal when the guard came strolling up to us. We will be executed next month.

Sally Watson (10)
Loretto Junior School, Musselburgh

Going For Gold

We were lined up ready to start, the sun blazing down on us. We all were eager to win. The starter fired his gun and we went sprinting towards the line, the people of Athens cheering us on. As I neared the finish line I tripped and there was a massive 'argh' from the crowd. I didn't let it affect me. I got back up and continued the race. I was in third position with a small distance to make up. I sprinted as fast as I could and won. My dream came true! I won gold.

Samuel Mukherjee (10)
Loretto Junior School, Musselburgh

The Diary Of Alina Clarke

18th March, 1940. I left everything behind when I stepped onto this train. Even my family. It's all because of this stupid war. My mother says that I'm lucky and should be happy that I've been evacuated though all I feel is a hollow emptiness. The train that I'm on has just stopped in Devon and I find Mrs Lightwood who'll take me in until the war is over.
19th March, 1940. Mrs Lightwood lives in a small farm cottage. I'm happy here though I miss my mother terribly. I want to go home. Mrs Lightwood is calling me now.

Eleanor Talbot (11)
Loretto Junior School, Musselburgh

The Battle Of Stirling Bridge

'Right, everyone ready? We need to form a schiltron and then we'll be able to defeat them,' I said. I have been training myself and all of my men. I will fight my hardest to win the battle.
'Sir, our enemy is here,' said Andrew.
'Brilliant, have they come to be crushed?' I said. 'Right everyone, get to the middle of the bridge, quick! Then form the schiltrons.'
The English army strode onto the bridge. They've lots of cavalry so our plan would work. We stabbed the whole army off the bridge. The English army were defeated.

Oliver Mukherjee (10)
Loretto Junior School, Musselburgh

Helicopter Ride Round The World

One day I got asked to go on a helicopter ride round the world. Later that day when I stepped into the tiny helicopter, we explored Asia. We flew over Russia then we went to Syria. I didn't like it because of the war. 'We nearly got shot down. Pilot!' I shouted. After that we went to Australasia. First we went to Uluru. It was tiny! Then we flew all the way to Africa. First we went to Tunisia. It was beautiful. Then we went to America. We went to Honduras. It was fantastic. Then we ran out of fuel...

Jamie Barker (9)
Loretto Junior School, Musselburgh

Balloon Ride!

One day there were two kids, Freya and Imaan, playing outside in their garden. They lived in Brazil near the rainforest but they absolutely hated the rainforest. One day they saw people go on a hot air balloon. Freya said, 'That looks fun, shall we go?'
'OK,' said Imaan, 'let's go.'
They made their very own hot air balloon and flew and flew up in the air. They had never been so high before and couldn't believe that they could actually see the whole of Brazil. They loved their hot air balloon but fell into the rainforest, feeling very scared.

Imaan Zaidi (8)
Loretto Junior School, Musselburgh

Stranded In The Bermuda Triangle!

I woke up. I heard waves. I saw some skeletons in a boat. They came over, shining a torch in my face. I backed away but they got me. I screamed, 'Help, help!' They took me to their boat to sail out of here. They told me we were in the Bermuda Triangle. I screamed again. 'Let's go!' We tried to drive away but it felt like the sea was eating us and it was doing it quickly. All the other people behind us were getting eaten and their boats too. I got out of the boat. I was stranded.

Grace Crawford (9)
Loretto Junior School, Musselburgh

Rorilandia!

Jeff, Bob and Uncle Phil were chasing Mop the dog. It was a teensy dog though it had a large amount of hair. The door opened. Mop smashed into the door with a crash, bang, wallop. It was only the postman. He had a letter for all of us. Uncle Phil opened the card. *Zoom!* Phil was falling quicker than you can say 'hip hip hooray'. He smacked his face on the dusty sand. 'Where are we?' shouted Jeff.

No one replied. Jeff saw a tree and Phil climbed it. He noticed a herd of wild buffalo approaching. 'Uh oh.'

Rory Lang (8)
Loretto Junior School, Musselburgh

Iceland Attack!

One day I woke up and turned on the radio. 'Breaking news, Iceland has grown and taken over Greenland,' blurted the man on the radio.

'Wow! If only we could do something!' I said to Poppy, my rabbit.

Eight centuries later... 'Breaking news,' boomed the man on the hologram, 'Iceland has taken over Norway.'

'Ooh, my back,' I said. 'Time to get that liver replacement to keep me alive.'

The next day Iceland was at my front doorstep. No seriously, it was on my front door. I saw evil Mr Iceland come out with a microphone and scream, 'Mwhahahaha!'

Ollie Shanks (8)
Loretto Junior School, Musselburgh

Mummy Vs Tony

On a cold and windy night Tony woke up early because of the wind. He couldn't get back to sleep so he tried to watch TV but couldn't. He went outside and said to the wind politely, 'Please go away,' but it didn't. He went back inside. The next day a mummy came and knocked on the door but he never answered. She knocked again and again. She knocked again so Tony answered the door and the mummy started a fight. The mummy was angry because she nearly died. A while later Tony jumped into a boat.

Morgan Forgie (7)
Meethill School, Peterhead

Viking Facts

Odin was a Viking. He was thinking that his children would take place of himself so he asked the tree of wisdom named Yggdrasil. The tree spoke. 'You will get wisdom if you give me your eye.'
He did and that's how Odin lost his eye.

Olek Kulczyk (9)
Meethill School, Peterhead

The Viking And Pirate

All of the Vikings wanted to attack. A Viking and a pirate wanted to hurt each other. Soon they liked each other and they became friends. They went to attack other people in another village. The villagers were scary and strong. The pirate and the Viking were so scared and didn't want to fight so they went on the Viking's longship to go to the Viking lands.

Evangeline Vanwyk (7)
Meethill School, Peterhead

World War

Boom! Crash! Kaboom! The war stopped. Jimmy hit an enemy soldier with his tank. The war started suddenly again all because of Jimmy. Another battle on the 2nd battleground. Jimmy was a tank commander and was a general and a super commander. He would capture anything that belonged to any enemy. On the way back to the battle, tanks were blown up and soldiers were killed and blown up. Finally the good soldiers won the war.

Ryan Dow (8)
Meethill School, Peterhead

The Death Of A Viking

Pirates sailed their way to the beach and saw Viking treasures. They attacked and fought. They saw a zombie and some other zombies were crawling from the ocean. The zombies stole the ship and sailed the seven seas. Captain Hook killed Viking Vikter and he died on the beach.

Erica-Leigh Davidson (8)
Meethill School, Peterhead

The Viking Saga

The Vikings were in Norway. The butcher cut the pig to eat. An enormous longship was built and a longhouse was built. The Vikings sailed to England, then they raided Peterhead. The people on Peterhead killed the Vikings. Then Thor waved his hammer and then thunder came. Then the Vikings roared and sliced the heads off the humans. Then the Swedish Vikings fought the Norwegian Vikings. Danish people came and defeated Sweden. The Peterhead men attacked the Vikings.

Danielius Babicius (8)
Meethill School, Peterhead

The Bunny

There was a little girl named Sophie and she loved bunnies or rabbits, and she really, really, really wanted one. Every day she went outside to find one but she never found one. One day she really found... oh no, it's just a cat. She'd not found one. 'Maybe tomorrow.' Wait! She saw a snow bunny. A magic bunny! The bunny had to go, it'd been out too long. Later, her mum got her one. Sophie named it Snow Bunny; she loved her snow bunny.

Nicole McGee (8)
Meethill School, Peterhead

Tony The Viking's Adventure

Tony and the Vikings wanted a battle. Tony can be silly sometimes. So they went to other places to find out if they wanted to have a battle because they were bored. Tony said, 'Do you want to have a battle?'
One person said, 'Yes, I do want to have a battle with you. We'll win because we're better!'
'No, we're better because you're scared.'
'No I'm not,' said the person.
They had a battle.

Megan Ovenstone (7)
Meethill School, Peterhead

The Vikings

On a sunny day I was in Peterhead shopping and then Morgan came along. Morgan said, 'Would you like to go for a walk on the hills?'

'I can't, sorry.'

'Okay, bye.'

'Sorry, Morgan.'

She went home and I did too. Then Vikings came to the door. They ran in and stole all my money and stuff and then ran out the door. I phoned Morgan and said, 'Help!'

'Chloe, what's the matter?'

'Vikings came to the door and stole my stuff and money.'

'Come to mine, we will talk about it!'

Chloe Plant (8)
Meethill School, Peterhead

The Great Wall Of China

Back in the year 206BC there was an emperor called Qin Shi Huang who decided to build a wall round the borders of China. The invaders like the Mongols were invading China so the emperor made the wall thirty-three foot tall and fifteen foot wide. They made thousands of lookout towers where soldiers could guard and protect his empire. Qin Shi Huang made horrible punishments for the ones who disobeyed the emperor. The punishments were being hanged, whipped, put in jail or removing an eye, or tongues, breasts or ears just cut off. Nobody ever disobeyed their emperor again.

Cerys Stuart (10)
Mosstodloch Primary School, Fochabers

Revelation

One day Thomas Telford went to Loch Ness. It was amazing! All he saw were small boats. *Kabing!* He thought how much people would appreciate his new idea. It sounded fabulous! 'I must make this canal.' He rushed back home.

Meanwhile, Rufus and Walrus were drinking whiskey when Thomas came in, all excited. 'Thomas! Come in, sit down,' said Rufus.

'No I can't. I'm going to make blueprints.'

After a few weeks he made the blueprints. Walrus helped all around the loch, building. After five months of intense labour and biting deadlines, they did it! Thomas was pleased with everyone!

Magnus Campbell (11)
Our Lady's RC Primary School, Perth

Thomas' Adventures

One day Thomas Telford was playing with his friends. He was having so much fun until, 'Argh!' Luke screamed. They started to run because evil monkeys were chasing them. Thomas gave Finn his spear. The rest of them chucked any natural materials into the river; sticks, stones, a log! Five minutes later the bridge was done. They all ran across. When they were all at the other side they destroyed the bridge so the evil monkeys could not get across. In the end they were all safe and the forest was banned.

Dominic Bews (10)
Our Lady's RC Primary School, Perth

The Fight Of The Titanic Ticket

April 4th, 1912.
As I was heading to buy a ticket for the Titanic, I saw the best and most dangerous thief ever. His name was... The Shadow. I quickly bought my ticket and ran away. He saw me and then stole my ticket to the Titanic. I stole it off him, but then he got so angry and he shot me in the arm and took my ticket. I got dizzy and fell down to the ground. I ended up in hospital and I couldn't go on the Titanic. My dreams died.

Karol Wieliczko (10)
Riverside Primary School, Stirling

Titanic

It was a calm, peaceful night when we hit something large. The crew said it was okay yet we ran to a lifeboat. Simon slipped on ice and almost fell off. I quickly grabbed him but he couldn't hold on and he fell, screaming at the top of his lungs. He soon stopped when he landed on a lifeboat but he suffered a broken spine. I jumped after him. As we slowly drifted away, the screams and cries and music slowly faded away before complete silence...

Jack Allan (10)
Riverside Primary School, Stirling

The Tragedy

I woke up very warm, like I'd been burnt by an inferno. I climbed up the fourth funnel to cool down and smoke a cigarette luxuriously. Suddenly I heard a bell ring. I saw what looked like an ice mountain. I thought we'd safely dodged it but we'd scraped the side of it! Then 3-2-1 *smash*, part of the iceberg was on Titanic's deck! I picked up a piece of the ice and held it in my hand. I quickly realised I wasn't going to make it. I knew I would never see my family ever again. I said goodbye.

Finlay Barr (10)
Riverside Primary School, Stirling

A Tragedy That Won't Be Forgotten

The bell rang and my heart stopped beating, I knew we were going down. The screaming was deafening as I got my life jacket on and ran down the grand staircase. Everyone was panicking and pushing to get to a lifeboat. My friend just got tipped overboard and her last words were, 'Save yourself, Ariana but please, always remember me!' At this point the shouting was getting too much, it was turning into a moment that would forever be a part of history. It was too late, the lifeboats were gone. I knew it was the end...

Erin Spence (10) & Katie Reilly (10)
Riverside Primary School, Stirling

War In The Trenches

On July 28th 1914, Great Britain went against Germany in World War I. Both sides had to go and stay in the horrible dirty trenches. War raged for four years and three months. There were over thirty-eight million soldiers who would come out of the trenches with their guns and the war would begin. When soldiers had bad injuries it was most likely that they would not survive as they could not get well treated for it in the trenches. In the end Great Britain won the war.

Dannika Leask (11)
Sound Primary School, Shetland

No-Man's-Land

On December the 24th 1914 war was still going strong and it was a scary sight.
The next day it was so quiet, almost too quiet. Just before they got their guns ready, the British saw a German soldier. The German soldier had a football. He said, 'Möchtest du fußball spielen?' which means, 'Do you want to play football?'
All of the British soldiers knew what that meant so they replied, 'Ja, ich würde gerne spielen, weil es weihnachten ist.' So they made goals out of jackets and they played so, so happily… until war broke out again.

Kara Grant (11)
Sound Primary School, Shetland

The Unexpected Escape

It was a fine day in the 1900s and Anna was off to feed Otto, just like her mother had asked her to. However, when Anna got there the gate was wide open and Otto was nowhere to be seen! It took Anna two and a half hours to find Otto. She eventually found him in the farmhouse kitchen, eating a lovely fresh apple pie that her mother had made. Anna had no idea what to do. She picked up the pie and ran to Otto's pen. She threw the pie and Otto ran in after it.

Lucy Kerr (11)
Sound Primary School, Shetland

The Allosaurus Chase

A lone ceratosaurus wanders into a giant allosaurus who is stalking him. The allosaurus snaps a branch with its foot. The ceratosaurus turns its head, it sees the allosaurus and starts to run. The allosaurus uses its big legs and easily catches up with him. It clamps its massive jaws on the ceratosaurus' neck. The ceratosaurus lets out a deafening scream. The allosaurus won't let go of the ceratosaurus' neck. There is so much blood spraying out of the wound. The ceratosaurus falls to the ground and moves around for a bit but it dies.

Keegan Watt (11)
Sound Primary School, Shetland

The Last Of The Stuarts

James V died of a disease and James VI became the King of Scotland and new King of England. When James VI became king he wanted to make a flag with Scotland and England so he made a flag called the Union Jack with blue, red and white colours. He made the flag fully complete. Soon he had a daughter. Before he could see her he died of old age. He never saw his daughter and that was the last of the Stuarts… or was it?

Dylan Hunter (11)
Sound Primary School, Shetland

The Nazis Attack!

Hitler lost WWI so he started WWII! So they all had a discussion about the war and then soon it started! Hitler hated the Jews and wanted to kill them all. He was the most evil person in human history. All of the wars were not just dangerous they were very dangerous and very scary. In WWII the soldiers got a thousand lice.
On Christmas Day they played a game of football and the next day they went back to war. All the people were scared, especially the Jews.

Jack Duncan (11)
Sound Primary School, Shetland

World War I

One freezing day Germany was going to battle with Britain. They had trenches they had to go in. They went in and got their guns ready. Hitler was the leader of the Germans. The leader of the British army was Winston Churchill. They went to fight. It was a brilliant fight and over 35 million soldiers died. At the end of the Battle of Britain it was all over for the Germans. You can guess who won. The Brits!

Ally Morrison (10)
Sound Primary School, Shetland

The Boat To Slavery

Mason and Mark sat huddled in the corner of the boat, waiting for the horrific day to come, wondering why they had to go into slavery. That was the last thing Mason thought as he died from shock. Mark could never survive this on his own. As Mark thought about Africa he cried. Life would never be the same again…

Fern Semple (10)
Sound Primary School, Shetland

The Never-Ending World War II

All you could hear were screams and bombs. We hid in the basement, I was shaking with fear. They'd beat us only because we're Jews. I thought of what might happen next.

It was a month later and we were still in hiding. Then one of the Nazis charged in and took me and my family. We were put in the concentration camp. Mum and Dad died after a beating; it was just me and my little brother, Ollie. Mum had said, 'Hope, you and Ollie will survive. I love you.'

Now it's safe, we're well and in care.

Lulu Johnson (10)
Sound Primary School, Shetland

The Black Hand

Captain Klaw and his crew got aboard the Red Flag. Jack Smith would've been left behind if his friend Billy Jones hadn't noticed him. The ship started to move. The captain told them they would move to find more ships to raid. Billy had had too much of raids, day after day. Most of the crew agreed with him. Jack had been making flags for Billy because he was the most experienced.
One day they walked up to Klaw and threw him overboard and now the ship was called the Black Hand.

Ciaran Leask (12)
Sound Primary School, Shetland

The Scarab Necklace

I began to lose my breath but I had to keep running. The guards were catching up! I had managed to fool them into thinking I was rich so I could steal the scarab necklace but escaping was a different matter. I ran around a corner trying to lose them for a while. Suddenly, the scarab started to glow then I shrunk. I was a beetle! I looked down and the necklace had shrunk down too and it turned into an eye. I scurried away, then touched the eye and I turned back into myself. *That's all today,* I thought.

Jenna Black (11)
Sound Primary School, Shetland

The Tomb

Diary entry twenty-eight - 5.6.1829.
Finally we've made it! It has taken us twenty-eight days to travel to Egypt from Paris but now me and my trusty companion, Ted, are here, raiding the tomb of Tutankhamun!
'Master, whatever shall we do?' cried Ted.
'Well, what do you do when you are stuck in a pitch-black room right underneath Tutankhamun's tomb?' asked Monsieur. Ted fell silent. 'You dig up!' Just as they started to dig, sand started to seep in!
Ted started to sob. 'Wait! That's not sand, that's gold!'

Isla Murphy (12)
Sound Primary School, Shetland

Agent Bjorn's Mission

'Agent Bjorn reporting for duty! I'm closing in through the forest.'
Bjorn the Great met the first of many enemy Vikings. They
weren't hard to defeat. With one blow Bjorn took the man's head
clean off. 'Easy,' muttered Bjorn.
Minutes later men were dying right, left and centre. As he walked
into the town of Skaagard he caught eyes with his sworn enemy,
Gamly the Ruthless. They started fighting, Gamly with a sword
and Bjorn with a battleaxe and tomahawks. After some time
things got brutal. Bjorn threw a tomahawk, it landed in Gamly's
bloody forehead. Mission accomplished.

Jordan Leask (12)
Sound Primary School, Shetland

The Mummy...

Once there was a mummy who was in his coffin for thousands of
years and a handsome man called Wayne came into the sphinx.
He saw the tomb and opened it. Seeing the mummy, he tried to
burn him. It didn't work. He got sucked into its stomach.
Afterwards, he roamed the streets, killing everything at night. A
nerd called Jordan thought that the mummy could die in the sun
and turn into ash. And so, the handsome Wayne was back and
he now went to a pyramid. This time he found riches.

Wayne Leask (12)
Sound Primary School, Shetland

The Trenches

'Lieutenant Morrison, Lieutenant Young,' the first officer said, 'you're going over the top! Go, go, go!' he yelled.
'Okay Sir,' we replied. We climbed out of our trench and ran across No-Man's-Land. Our men were falling like trees all around us. We realised that we would be next! 'Quick hide here!' A small tree was standing in the middle of No-Man's-Land. We dived on the ground and hid until dark, when we sneaked over to the German trench. The guards had fallen asleep. We jumped into the trench and stole their guns. The trench was ours!

Matthew Spence (11)
Sound Primary School, Shetland

The Bomb At The Butcher

Ellie was walking with Lizzie down to the butcher's when suddenly the screechy air raid went off, it was a false alarm. They went back in line and waited.
When they were walking back home an air raid went off. This time it wasn't a false alarm and they ran away as far as they could. Jumping into someone's garden they hid under a tree. The air raid went on for ages. It was dark. Someone came out the door. When they looked at the man he was the Prime Minister, Winston Churchill.

Lotti Rendall (11)
Sound Primary School, Shetland

The Run Through The Blitz!

Mother told Helen, Ruth and I we were to go fill up the water buckets. We each took a bucket and went on our way. We walked all the way to the town which took a while. When we got to the tap we filled up the water, then we heard a big boom. We heard lots of them. We realised they were bombs, so we ran as fast as we possibly could. We were so scared, we didn't even stop to catch our breath. We saw our cottage, we ran in and realised we'd left behind the water buckets.

Estella Smith (11)
Sound Primary School, Shetland

John The Great

This is about John the Great, a Viking who stole and fought with innocent people.
One day, John the Great had a longship and said to his army, 'Let's go steal the land. There's gold.' So they did! They sailed for two hours and reached their destination. John attacked and stole from the people in the village and set it on fire. When they were sailing back enemy Vikings came and sunk their longship and stole all the goods. John quickly swam back and told the awful tale and John the Great was great again…

Ellie Bisset (11)
Sound Primary School, Shetland

The Christmas Truce

It all started one cold morning when the Germans woke up to the smelly, muddy trenches. Germans heard sweet singing from the Brits. 'It's Silent Night!' They got up from their restless sleep and sung it in German. They all came together and had a truce. A German soldier and a British soldier walked up to each other. 'My name is Peter.'
'My name is Tom.' They became best friends until the truce was over. They both survived the war and wrote letters to each other. It shows you that a truce can change everything, even in war.

Zoe Semple (11)
Sound Primary School, Shetland

Tom And The Shetland Bus

Tom was sailing across to Norway on the Shetland Bus. Tom was a fisherman but since the war had started his boat had been turned into the Shetland Bus. Tom arrived in Norway; he had to find the prison. As he reached the prison and told them who he was, the prisoners became very excited. They went back to the Shetland Bus and all got on; it was difficult for them to fit. When they were halfway across the ocean a German U-boat came across the horizon. I'm sad to say that everybody on the boat died.

Freya Laurenson (11)
Sound Primary School, Shetland

A Saboteur's Run

It started off fine; the maiden voyage had begun, it wasn't a happy voyage for long. Connor Watts went onto the ship to follow an industrial saboteur, John Harwins. This man took down Connor's business in a week.

Days went by and the Titanic was struck! Everyone rushed to the lifeboats. Connor confronted John on the bow of the ship. John ripped off a metal pipe to use to attack Connor. A giant pipe fell and crushed John! Connor rushed to the last lifeboat and jumped into it. The RMS Titanic sank into the dark, blue ocean.

Xander Souter (12)
Sound Primary School, Shetland

The Ancient Architect

There was once a boy called Seti, he lived in Egypt. He was an architect who designed pyramids.

One day Seti was starting work on a new pyramid and he said to his builders, 'Put that brick there. And you, with the yellow shorts, put that brick there.' Seti examined the blueprint very carefully to make sure every brick was place correctly. Once the pyramid was finally finished he looked up at the pyramid and stared in astonishment. 'The pyramid is upside down, I was looking at the blueprint upside down!' Seti never lived to tell the tale.

Vinessa Carr
Sound Primary School, Shetland

Heroes

'I can hear the bombs falling, they sound horrific,' said Calum.

'Horrifically scary,' replied Mark.

'Scaredy cat, scaredy cat,' chanted Calum.

'Get under the table now!' shouted Mark.

Boom!

'A bomb dropped on the neighbour's house,' whispered Mark, as he peered out the window.

'Let's go see if they're OK,' said Calum.

'What? Out there?'

'Yeah, where else? Come on.'

When they got there, their neighbours were lying among the rubble. They put them into a wheelbarrow which they found and ran as fast as they could to the hospital. They saved their lives and were now known as heroes.

Tahlia Leslie (11)
Sound Primary School, Shetland

Sold In Slavery

There I was, sitting in a dark, damp, small, eerie room. 'Jack, where are you?' I heard his voice crumbling like Mother's pie at home. I couldn't see anyone but I could hear their breath falling away. I was scared. So was Jack. 'Well, well, well, let's take you to Douglas.' I heard the next cellar open. The children began to scream. Crying, terrified is what they were. It gave me the shivers. Then I heard the coarse voice of a helper. He opened our cell. I saw the shimmer of metal. Was this the end?

Jessie Jamieson (10)
Sound Primary School, Shetland

The Boy In The Larder

'Mother, may I go for a walk?' asked Lady Grace.
'Of course,' replied her mother.
Off she went, strolling along the street. Suddenly, she bumped into a lonely, struggling boy. 'Are you alright?' she asked.
'No!' shouted the boy.
I will help him, she thought to herself. Ad she did!
Years passed and the little boy still lived in the fancy Victorian girl's larder until one day her mother reached her hand into the larder to grasp a couple of things. 'Argh!' she'd grasped a hand. Although, the boy had to leave, Lady Grace vowed to help him.

Laura Bisset (11)
Sound Primary School, Shetland

In The Gladiator's Ring

Zeke and Zachariah were sitting around the fire discussing their plans to kill Julius Caesar. 'We'll push him into the gladiators' ring tomorrow,' said Zachariah.
'Let's do it!' said Zeke.
The next day Zeke was in the ring and Zachariah was hiding behind the emperor's box. Julius Caesar came in. Zachariah tried to make himself invisible. Zeke was on in the ring. Zachariah waited and he pushed Caesar so hard that he fell into the ring with the lion and Zeke. Caesar rose. He took them to his palace to cover them in horse poo in the palace courtyard.

Laurie Morris (11)
Sound Primary School, Shetland

The Lost Child

Many moons ago, in the town of London, Germany started to invade. They called it the Blitz. The Smith family were trying to get to an air raid shelter. To do this they needed to go through the Underground. While the Smith family were walking through they saw a little boy. He was crying his eyes out as he had lost his mother. The Smith family felt very badly for this little boy, he was going to get hurt. The family took him to the air raid shelter and he was safe.
The next day he found his worried mother.

Sarah Louise McAllister (12)
Sound Primary School, Shetland

The German Castle

The Blitz hit so we had to leave London for the countryside. There was a gas attack on the train and I was knocked unconscious. As the train gathered speed, I woke up. I was soon in a castle. The owner looked suspicious and told me never to go down to the castle's basement. I was curious so at midnight I snuck down to the basement. I heard a voice. People were speaking in German. I saw at least five people including the owner. I wrote down what they said. 'I must warn Mr Churchill. But will I escape?'

Ryan Peart (11)
Sound Primary School, Shetland

Mary Queen Of Scots' Gory Death

'Please,' Mary pleaded, 'let me go.'

'No!' shouted Elizabeth.

'Ready your Highness?' asked the executioner.

'Yes,' replied Elizabeth.

'No!'

Chop!

Mary screamed, her shoulder had been taken off instead of her head. 'Argh!'

'Be quiet, you brat!' screamed Elizabeth. 'Try again but do it properly this time.'

'OK, sorry Mary.'

'Don't be sorry!' shouted Queen Elizabeth, in total fury.

Chop!

'It's done,' said Elizabeth, 'it's over.'

The executioner screamed.

'What, what is it?'

'Her lips are twitching.'

'Eww, hit it with your axe!'

'No way!'

'I, the Queen, order you to.'

Whack!

'She is dead.'

'I, Elizabeth, declare this over.'

Emma Leask (12)
Sound Primary School, Shetland

The Saga Of Jack Black

The crew reached their ship, the Hellbound, with looks of happiness on their faces, like a pair of gleeful children. They boarded their ship but Captain Jorund took the treasure from the monastery and kept it himself. The crew were fuming! Jack Black whispered one word: 'Mutiny,' to Oddlog, Meldon, Magnus and Karl.

Later, at night, they attacked the captain but before he died he said, 'So I see why you never really had friends: you're a psycho.' Then with a swipe of a sword, he fell to the deck. His curse stuck with Jack always.

Johnathan Goudie (11)
Sound Primary School, Shetland

Christmas War

On September 1st, 1939, Germany attacked Poland. It caused havoc. The British declared war on Germany. Polish Jews fled from the major cities, like Warsaw and Krakow, to the country. When they were in all the small villages they heard the rumble of tanks. They thought it was the British and were relieved but when they came over the brows of hills it was a Nazi invasion! There were three trucks filled with cavalry, tanks and some motorbikes with side-cars; they took over the village. They punished the Jews and made them sad.

Ethan Dunn (10)
Sound Primary School, Shetland

The Battle Of Time

Once in Northern America there was a town of cowboys who lived peacefully. One day they heard rumbling under their feet so ran into their homes for safety. They realised it was the Romans who came from the past to attack them and take over America. The first village they came to was the village Travis the sheriff lived in. Travis came out of his house and the first enemy he saw was Alba, the Roman warrior. They had a big fight, cowboys versus Romans. The Romans got defeated and the cowboys celebrated by eating their best food.

Christian Thomas Anderson (10)
Sound Primary School, Shetland

The Gunpowder Plot

Guy Fawkes and the rest of the plotters were getting ready to kill King James. Guy Fawkes was chosen to go down to the basement and stay there until he had to light the gunpowder. The guards came down to the basement to check everything and what they found was Guy Fawkes. They took him and tortured him until he told them where the others were. All of the plotters were found and were sentenced to be hanged, drawn and quartered on the 31st of January 1606.

Eve Fraser (10)
Sound Primary School, Shetland

War For Days

My name is General Jeff. Today we went to war for the third time this week. I hate the trenches so much, they smell of my brother's feet and the lice are so itchy and sore. Now we're climbing out of them to No-Man's-Land where the Germans are shooting and throwing grenades. A German is running at me so I am shooting him. He is dead. We are still shooting them and they are shooting us. Now the Germans are retreating. We have won the war. I will celebrate by drinking lots of beer.

Finn Regan (10)
Sound Primary School, Shetland

Preparing For Wicked War

It was the day before World War II started and there were lots of men flying out to the battlefields and trenches. At an airport in London, a plane was getting ready to leave and all the soldiers were getting ready to board. It was a British plane and it was heading to the battlefields. Hitler was leading the Germans and Winston Churchill was leading the British. Hitler was trying to kill all of the Jews. Most of the Jews had left the major cities and gone to villages in the country. The British were going to defend them. Britain won!

Liam Robbie Slater (10)
Sound Primary School, Shetland

Untitled

'What?'

'Mum's been captured.'

'OK, I don't really care.'

'But she's been taken to England to be beheaded!'

'I still don't care, as long as I'm alive it's OK.'

Later that month; *Ding-dong, ding-dong!*

'What happened?'

'Your mum's dead.'

'OK, now I'm scared, I didn't think it would really happen!'

A few months of hiding in the cupboard later… 'Queen Elizabeth's dead! Yaaay! Congratulations James, you're King of England and Scotland.'

'What should I call this place since we're together now?'

'I know Sir. How about the United Kingdom?'

'Marvellous idea. You can go now.'

Hayley Moar (11)
Sound Primary School, Shetland

The Temple

It all began when I was a young man with a job as a guard.
My cousin, Stephen, was engaged to his boss, Sally Thunder. He told me that it's not weird to be engaged to your boss.
The next day, I was reading a book when Stephen and Sally came in, all battered and bruised. 'What on Earth is going on here?' I asked.
'The king's guards are after us,' replied Stephen. Just then, six spears came through the window and nearly took off my head! Then the wall fell down. I was standing next to it as it fell.

Hayden Fraser (9)
Sound Primary School, Shetland

The Romans Vs Native Americans

One day the Romans found new land. The Roman king was happy with his new land but the Native Americans were living on the land. King Thor rallied his army to attack the natives under the cover of darkness. The war was violent and bloody with the Native Americans being victorious and saving their homeland. The Romans were taken as slaves and King Thor was executed. As time passed they learned to live together in peace and they lived happily ever after.

Jason Campbell (12)
Sound Primary School, Shetland

A Twist In Time

Once upon a time, two triceratops were playing on a hill and they tumbled down it plunging into a black hole. When they looked around, it wasn't home! A voice said, 'What are you doing here?' They looked up and there in front of them was a tall lady with hair that looked like fire. 'What are your names?'
'We don't have any and we don't know why we are here?'
'Oh!' said Boudicca. 'Your names will be Sydney and Sara. We will build a time machine to get you home!'
After quite some time, Sydney and Sara returned home.

Eloise March (9)
Sound Primary School, Shetland

The Masterpiece

One day the wizard was mixing up his potions when the emperor burst through the doors. 'Could you help me?' the emperor shouted.
'I need you and the artist to make a masterpiece for the grand opening in one week. Quickly!'
'Alright,' replied the wizard.
'Thank you,' said the emperor, relieved.
So the wizard ran to the artist's house 'Quick!' he said. 'The emperor needs us to make up a picture for the grand opening in one week!'
'OK, we'd better get started right away!' he said. That's just what they did…

Ellie Chapman (8)
Sound Primary School, Shetland

Ancient Adventure

Once there lived a soldier called Boudicca. She was a girl and could beat ten men on her own. She was the best soldier.
One day one of the guards saw thousands of people coming to attack the village. Boudicca was so frightened she ran away. Suddenly, she fell in an underground tunnel. She shouted so much but nobody heard her. She looked around and saw a little bunny that was cold and hungry. Then she saw a rope so she threw it up, climbed out and ran back to the village.

Brooke Leslie (8)
Sound Primary School, Shetland

Ancient Adventure

Once upon a time in Ancient Rome, there were two best friends called Camal and Camar. They were servants to the emperor and the emperor made them work so hard.
One day, they gave the emperor the wrong food. The emperor was furious and ordered them to battle to the death with each other.
Camal and Camar were terrified of hurting each other, so had to think up a way to stop the fight happening.
On the day of the fight the two men pretended to fight each other but suddenly turned towards the emperor and killed him.

Ashleigh Calderwood (9)
Sound Primary School, Shetland

The Dark Hole

A long time ago there lived a wolf called Buster. Buster was an angry wolf because he felt lonely and picked on by the rest of the pack.

Buster dreamt of going back in time to meet Loki and Thor, the great Viking gods, Buster's heroes.

Buster discovered a special hole which made his foot invisible. Perhaps it was a black hole? He jumped in the hole, made a wish and went to the other side. To his surprise, two strange, tall men welcomed him. Was it Loki and Thor or somebody else?

Adam Card (8)
Sound Primary School, Shetland

World War II

It was 1939 and World War II had started. Hitler, the leader of Germany, hated Jewish people and only liked people who were non-Jewish and had blond hair and blue eyes. Germany had lots of Jews that they had captured and put in concentration camps for them to work for Hitler.

Britain marched forward, taking over lots of Germany and started to gain ground. Then Hitler and his family committed suicide and Britain won the war; Germany surrendered.

Aaron Regler (11)
Sound Primary School, Shetland

King Charles' Royal Rage

One day in London 1666 King Charles was sitting on his throne when a servant approached him and said, 'There is a great fire going on here in London and it's approaching us.'
'What?' he replied furiously. 'Stop it then!' Anger grew inside the king. The servant thought the king looked stressed so he ordered the jester to come and cheer him up. He saw the jester and almost exploded with anger; he ran towards the jester rugby tackling him to the ground before sprinting out of his palace and diving straight into the River Thames.

Sonny Teale (12)
Sound Primary School, Shetland

The Story Of Queen Elizabeth

Once upon a time there lived Queen Elizabeth I and her husband James. The queen liked to walk around the castle grounds. She was walking around the pond when suddenly she fell into some mud which turned out to be magical mud! She began to shrink. She was green and slimy! 'I'm turning into a frog!' she cried. She hopped back down to the castle to get help from her husband. 'Oh dear!' The queen worried.
James and his brother, Jordan, were going for a walk when James stepped on a rather beautiful frog…
Poor Queen Elizabeth was flattened. *Splat!*

Kelsey Neill (8)
Sound Primary School, Shetland

Roman Times

One day, long ago, a Roman child was playing with his mum outside in their garden. Roman soldiers grabbed the boy's mum and killed her with a sword. The little boy was taken prisoner. John, a kind man, heard the boy crying in the prison cell. John had a special power: he could change into any animal he wanted. He turned himself into a huge dinosaur and used his tail to smash open the prison gate.

The boy was terrified! John quickly changed back into a man. The boy went to live with John for the rest of his life.

Sebastian Nicol (8)
Sound Primary School, Shetland

Germans Arrive

Once there were two little boys called James and Mark. One day, they were attacked by Germans.

Mark and James were scared. 'I'm scared,' said Mark.

I'm scared too, thought James. 'I hope Dad helps us!'

'I hope we don't die!' cried Mark.

'Me too,' replied James.

'Hide, I see a German!' said Mark.

'Hide, hide…'

Eventually the German left. 'That German had a sharp sword and a big bow,' observed Mark.

'It's Dad!' announced James. 'Yay, it's Dad!'

'Dad, we're here in the bedroom!' Dad found James and Mark.

'I'm so glad to see you boys!' Dad said excitedly.

Leland Wiseman (9)
Sound Primary School, Shetland

Stone Age Hurricane

Once upon a time there lived a Stone Age family: Toby, Roxy and their daughter, Mississippi.
One day, a ferocious hurricane came and devastated the land. The family were separated. Toby lost Roxy and Mississippi. He couldn't phone them in those days! Luckily, Roxy and Mississippi survived and bumped into an old friend who looked after them by giving them food, water and shelter. They played together and took care of one another. Surely it wouldn't be long until they were reunited with Toby?
Two years later, a trembling earthquake occurred, bringing the land and family together again at last.

Koby Sinclair (8)
Sound Primary School, Shetland

An Egyptian Saga

Long, long ago in a land far away, Egypt in fact, there lived an evil pharaoh. He was cruel to his hundreds of slaves. He whipped them, he beat them, he beheaded them. All he cared about was himself and the gigantic pyramid his poor slaves were building for his death.
One day, a poor slave called Robert thought, *I've had enough of this!* He got close to the pharaoh and managed to grab a spear from a soldier and stabbed the pharaoh in his head. Robert became the new pharaoh and freed all the slaves.

Isaac Ritchie (8)
Sound Primary School, Shetland

A Secret Fairy Garden Forever

Once upon a time there were fairies who lived in a secret garden. One day a new fairy arrived in town, her name was Natricia. When Aurora, Bella, Ellie, Lily, Rosie and Emily went to the library they read a book all about Natricia. The book told them that she wanted to steal everything that had the word 'secret' in it. The fairies didn't read all of the book so they didn't know that fairy Natricia had special powers and that she was planning to use these powers against them. The fairies found out in time and stopped her.

Neve Hogg (7)
St Aloysius Primary School, Airdrie

Titanic Love Story

It took three years to build the Titanic. The Titanic ship sailed from England to New York. Aboard there was a girl called Rose and a boy called Jack. Rose was posh but Jack was poor. They both met and they fell in love. They started to dance. They went to the very edge of the gigantic ship and Rose felt like she was flying. Then the ship started to wobble and crashed into an iceberg, the ship sank. Jack drowned but luckily Rose stayed alive. When a ship sinks it's called a shipwreck.

Mirabelle Tipping (9)
St Anthony's Primary School, Saltcoats

The Big Swim

Once upon a time in a house of two… 'Alfred!' shouted his mum. 'Look what's in the paper.'
'A new sport?'
'It's called swimming. It's on tonight, would you like to try it?'
'Erm, it's a competition,' said Alfred, looking worried. 'Oh okay, I'll go.' So off they went.
'Alfred look, the king is presenting the medals.' Alfred had never seen the king before. *Boom!* The gunshot sounded. Alfred was off. He saw a girl in front of him so he pushed to get to the finish. At that very moment the king shouted, 'Alfred wins gold!'

Rachel McGuire (9)
St Anthony's Primary School, Saltcoats

The First Breeze

'What just happened?' John gasped. Nobody answered. He looked around but all he could see was rows of tents… empty. John looked as if he was ready to cry but he was stopped as loud cries of a blizzard started nearby. He ran inside a large green tent. John sat in a sleeping bag in a daze. As he calmed he heard whimpers at the back of the tent. John sat still, waiting to see the creatures at the door. He saw one massive tooth and realised it was a sabre-toothed tiger. Its paw was injured but John loved him.

Calum Lynch (9)
St Anthony's Primary School, Saltcoats

William The Conqueror

'Why are people always trying to kill me?'
'Because, William, you are only seven and people want to take over your land.'
'Well I am going to grow up and be tough and one day I am going to conquer England.'
And so he did.
William's first battle was when he was just 19 and he died in his last battle at the age of 59. His last battle was in the town of Mantes in France.
'I was told he suffered for five weeks before he finally died.'
RIP William.

Abby Tolland (9)
St Anthony's Primary School, Saltcoats

Egyptian 2.0

There was once a nine-year-old boy called Jeff. The subject he was learning in school was the Egyptians. He didn't believe the stories were true. As Jeff gazed out the window, an army of pharaohs burst into the classroom. 'Jeff, we have come for you!' They yanked him and all of a sudden he was in Egypt. Next thing he was in an Egyptian prison. As he shook with fear, his teacher appeared at the other side of the bars. Staring at him, she said, 'The only way home is to believe.' *Bang!* Jeff woke up in his class.

Leah McColl (10)
St Anthony's Primary School, Saltcoats

The Titanic

A long time ago, the largest ship afloat set sail from Southampton for the first time ever. It was trying to get to New York City. It was a glorious day, what could go wrong? 'I think the inside of the ship will have chandeliers hanging from the ceiling and big, long tables in the dining room,' said a boy called Joe to his friend, Thomas. When they got on-board, what could go wrong?
That night the ship was sailing through icebergs and the Titanic hit one of them. It took two hours for the Titanic to sink.

Niamh Milne (9)
St Anthony's Primary School, Saltcoats

Zolo's First Fight

'Come back you numbskull!' shouted Kingo, the shopkeeper of Katana King. Zolo kept on running and headed straight for the ship with the new katana he stole.
'Did you steal another katana?' asked Captain Shanks.
'What do you think?' said Zolo.
'Come on then, we are going to Indonesia!' Zolo ran faster and made a huge leap. He landed on the edge of the ship. The ship headed straight for Indonesia.
Two days later, the ship smashed into the beach. 'Land ahoy!' Shanks and his crew jumped out. They ran and slashed their swords. Zolo bashed his katana.

Shon Thomas (11)
St Marie's Primary School, Kirkcaldy

Evacuation

'Kate! Run! It's very dangerous here!' shouted Kate's mum. The trains were full and it was freezing. Kate was so scared she didn't know where she was going. The journey was so long but finally she arrived. There were lots of people standing and waiting. She got out of the train and there was a man and a woman. They chose Kate. She couldn't say no. At least they were nice. They had one daughter called Eve who was really nice. They could play together. Now Kate lives in a nice house but will she ever see her parents again?

Natalia Podlesiecka (11)
St Marie's Primary School, Kirkcaldy

The Scraggly Stowaway

A captain and his crew, sailing on a dark night, found a
stowaway. Happy was her name. The captain kept her as his
own. They threw her a party and crowned her a pirate. She was
scraggly, young and needing a home. Then a brutal storm blew
the ship over. Would they survive? Nobody knew. Oh look, Happy
did. She tried to swim away but sank near to land. Suddenly, she
awoke in a comfy bed surrounded by… pirates! Hooray for her,
but were these pirates friend or foe? She'd have to find out when
she gained her strength back!

Emily Ferguson (11)
St Marie's Primary School, Kirkcaldy

The Massive Battle

'Fire!' Matthew heard his men further up the battlefield scream.
Suddenly, there was a round of shells fired and someone cried,
'We got them!' Joseph, the driver of Matthew's Sherman, stopped
when they reached the other tanks.
'Tiger,' Matthew whispered, 'everybody roll forward and flank from
the right and left.' Joseph circled the Tiger while Matthew was
manning the gun. Lots of shells were fired at the Tiger and it was
eventually destroyed, however, it'd taken out three of the five
Shermans. 'We lost quite a few men this time but next time we
will destroy them all.'

Daniel Martin (11)
St Marie's Primary School, Kirkcaldy

Leaving The One Place You Know As Home

'But I don't want to leave you!' cried Cara the moment the ship set sail to the middle of nowhere. 'I just don't want to…' Her voice trailed off into the fog. Cara spotted some others sitting under a ledge on the portside of the ship. She didn't recognise their faces from back on the island.

'Hello,' belted Bertha the Belter in Cara's direction. Cara instantly knew who it was.

'Hi there,' said a meek little voice from behind Bertha. 'I'm Savage the Non-Savage.'

They ended up talking for hours. As they were talking, 'Land ahoy!' was screamed.

Bryony McCormick (11)
St Marie's Primary School, Kirkcaldy

Hickup's Big Adventure

There once were four little Vikings called Hickup, Tomrad, Madagascar and Shuvelot. They wanted to go on an adventure to capture the crown jewel. They set off on their journey but when they looked on the map, the island wasn't there to be seen. With Hickup's brains he managed to get to the island but out of nowhere a troll came. Thankfully, with their skills they got it out of the way. There was the jewel! They took it and headed back home. When they arrived they saw an army taking away Hickup's dad, the king…

Evan Wishart (11)
St Marie's Primary School, Kirkcaldy

Queen Victoria's Scary Surprise

One day it was Queen Victoria's birthday and she wanted to invite everyone. She went out and everyone looked at her while she gave out invitations. Suddenly, she was absolutely excited. Her party awaited.

An hour later she was getting ready, the party was in twenty minutes. Her servants all around her tightened her dress, did her hair, adjusted her crown, and looked at her shoes. She was ready, just in time! When she arrived, it was pitch dark and the lights were going off. When the lights came back on nobody was there…

Emma-Louise Nisbet (11)
St Marie's Primary School, Kirkcaldy

Away For A Sail

'Welcome to my boat,' shouted Captain Redbeard.

On came Claus and Hiccup. 'Ahoy there,' screamed Hiccup, and off they set on their adventure. They saw lots of things but they were looking out for a small coconut island. They could not find it. It came to night-time and they all had to sleep on the boat in the atrocious weather in the freezing cold! 'Night,' said Hiccup. 'Night,' they both said back sounding worried.

In the morning they found the island and got the coconuts and then the boat floated away down the sea and disappeared…

Claire Nicholson (11)
St Marie's Primary School, Kirkcaldy

Stranded

The sky was getting dimmer as the pirates were sailing across the beautiful ocean… *Bang!* 'What was that?' screamed Jessica. 'It's a thunderstorm,' squealed Ryan.
'We are going to crash!' shouted everyone. *Crash!* Everyone woke up.
'Where are we?' said James.
'Looks like a desert island to me,' muttered Mark.
'We have to get items to build a raft to get off the island.'
'Erm, there is no wood on the island,' said Liam.
'Everyone calm down, we can still get water and food.'
'Crew, it looks like we are all stranded on this desert island!' shouted James.

Owen Thomson (11)
St Marie's Primary School, Kirkcaldy

The Annoying Egyptians

A long time ago, in Ancient Egypt, there was a king called King Atoot. He always liked to annoy people, even his dim servants. They liked it because they were used to it.
One day tourists came to Egypt, minding their own business, when King Atoot came and introduced himself by saying, 'Pull my finger.' So the tourists did and then King Atoot trumped and started laughing. Weirdly the tourists wanted peace and quiet but King Atoot just threw water balloons at them.
The tourists got back on the boat to America. 'Argh!' shouted the tourist. 'He's here!'

Kyle Barclay (11)
St Marie's Primary School, Kirkcaldy

The Germans Are Closing In!

In 1939, I was in the trenches. I had mud down my neck. I was freezing. Our captain had just told us that the Germans were closing in. Most of our troops had been shot dead. I felt like I was holding a suitcase full of rocks. I kept on tripping on mounds of mud and falling on my face every few minutes. My gun was so heavy and I had to pop up from the trench and shoot every few minutes. The last thing I remember was the sound of gunshots and blotches of blood on my arm.

Owen Parry (11)
St Marie's Primary School, Kirkcaldy

Dread Of Titanic

Suddenly, I heard a bang. I never worried though.
About five minutes later I got back to sleep but Mum woke me up immediately. She told me to put on all of my clothes. I got scared after I heard that Titanic had smashed into an iceberg. The crew members towed the lifeboats down. The crew member announced that women and children were to get on first. I stepped on the boat with Mum, sadly looking up at Dad. Luckily, we made it but Dad never did. I was so sad and never went on a cruise ship again…

Mark Robertson (11)
St Marie's Primary School, Kirkcaldy

The Battle!

'Nearly there!' said Roader.

'The home of the giants. Yes! I am here!' exclaimed Roader, five days later. *Thump! Thump! Thump!* 'What was that?' said Roader, scared.

'Get out of my land or else,' said the giant, Hymer.

'Or else what?' said Roader.

'I will fight you!' said Hymer.

'OK, let's do this!' said Roader.

The battle went on for hours until finally the winner was… Hymer! Then Hymer tossed Roader into the air and he was never heard of again, although his helmet landed in his Viking village…

James Whitelaw (9)
Strath Of Appin Primary School, Appin

Goblin Cove

One time in Asgard, Iduna was picking apples. It was 7.35pm, her bedtime. When she was sleeping some goblins came through her window and kidnapped her. Iduna woke feeling strange and mysterious. Her vision was blurry. She looked around and realised she was in Goblin Cove. She looked behind her and saw a goblin holding some water. Iduna took the water and drank it. She felt a lot better. She stayed for a bit. She went back to the castle and Odin and Loki were there. Iduna looked in the mirror… She was a goblin!

Jenny Whitelaw (9)
Strath Of Appin Primary School, Appin

Friendship

Rolf woke to horrific screams of death coming from the main streets of Jorvik! At first he thought he was dreaming, then he realised it was real. As fast as lightning he ran from the dark alley to the main deck. He clambered onto the longship and hid behind a drum. Then he saw his best friend, Timothy, getting thrown into a cage. He heard a voice saying, 'Rolf! Help me!' Rolf ran as fast as he could back to town. Rolf picked the cage lock. Timothy snuck out the cage. They ran and hid until the Vikings left.

Callan Taylor (9)
Strath Of Appin Primary School, Appin

The Sea Monster...

One day seventy Vikings went sailing in the nice, calm sea. The sun was shining. When the Vikings were in the middle of the sea they saw fourteen spikes in the water. All the Vikings shouted, 'Argh!' The beast didn't go away, instead it showed its head. it was a sea monster. The Vikings dropped their weapons. Only Redbeard didn't, he threw his sword and the sword hit the beast in the head. The monster died. All the Vikings cheered. 'Yay!' They sailed back, then had a really fun Viking party!

Duncan Cameron (8)
Strath Of Appin Primary School, Appin

The Great Warrior

In the dark wood Odihan, the Viking warrior, met a giant called Skymner. During the battle, Skymner blasted Odihan but he got right back onto his feet. He threw his double-sided sword at the giant! The giant started to bleed. 'Uh, you hit me right in the stomach!' Odihan ran to Skymner, ran up his leg, grasped his double-sided sword and backflipped off. He started running up Skymner. Odihan stabbed Skymner in the head. The earth shook when Skymner fell to the ground.

Jack Johnston (9)
Strath Of Appin Primary School, Appin

The Mysterious Wood

It was an ordinary day when Ivar Redbeard took Shaggy the dog for a walk. Suddenly, Shaggy ran away into a forest. Ivar looked for Shaggy then Ivar ended up in a mysterious place where the sun would never rise! Was Ivar still in the village? With his eyes peeled, he looked for Shaggy. Ivar still couldn't find him and it was getting late… Ivar heard an echoing bark and there was an animal sprinting towards him. Was it Shaggy? 'Shaggy!' he shouted. And you know what? It was Shaggy. Hooray! Now they had to find their way out!

Daisy Carmichael (8)
Strath Of Appin Primary School, Appin

Viking Trouble

In Asgard there was a little boy called Haraled. He was playing catch with his pet dog. He stopped for a moment and saw a massive shadow coming down the hill. He was just about to run when he noticed the massive shadow was Skrymir, the king of all the giants. It was Haraled's cousin Loki's party. Haraled wasn't there! They ran outside and all they could hear was screaming. His dad followed the screaming and he stabbed Skrymir with his magic sword. It was a fatal wound. His dad took Haraled and they ate some birthday cake.

Erin Claire Jackson (8)
Strath Of Appin Primary School, Appin

The Party

In Asgard the gods were getting ready for a party, celebrating Odin's 112th birthday! When all the guests were there Odin made an announcement. The first game was musical thrones. The winner was Iduna. The prize was 52 apples. Halfway through Iduna went missing. Loki told Thor to find who took her. Odin's birthday party turned into a search party! Thor saw the goblins and Vikings sneaking away with Iduna. He smashed them with his hammer, saved Iduna and returned her to the palace safely.

Ellie Hearnden (8)
Strath Of Appin Primary School, Appin

An Unforeseen Occasion Of Battle

Suddenly, all of the gods in Asgard heard a titanic stomp. The giants were approaching! The battle was on. Screams were echoing around the gods. Unexpectedly, the kingdom caught fire. Thor unleashed a gargantuan thundercloud. It started striking the giants but it didn't affect them. Odin knew they had magic, so he created an anti-magic forcefield. Randomly, the fire stopped. Thor's thundercloud stopped the fire. The giant's leader charged in with a shiny club, but it disappeared because it was a magic club. The gods and giants settled with the agreement of a truce. They never fought again.

Max Allen (9)
Strath Of Appin Primary School, Appin

The Magical Bunny

One sunny day Iduna was playing in the garden with Brynhild, a wild bunny. Loki was in a bush, spying on Iduna. Loki crept towards Iduna from the bush. 'Brynhild's my bunny!' shouted Loki. 'No, she's not!' Iduna replied.
'Let's have a challenge to decide who keeps Brynhild.'
'We'll both take care of her for half a day.'
'Fine,' said Loki.
Iduna took Brynhild for the morning and Loki took her for the afternoon. Loki and Iduna stood metres away from each other. 'Brynhild will choose,' said Iduna. Brynhild went to Iduna but disappeared in a blink of an eye.

Eva MacColl (10)
Strath Of Appin Primary School, Appin

The Flying Fish

Once the Vikings gods, Loki and Thor, went on an adventure. They got into Thor's chariot. When they got to Midgard they got out for a walk.

On their walk they met Viking Redbeard. Loki and Thor knew Redbeard, they were friends when Loki was younger. It was getting dark so they went home.

On the way home Loki shape-shifted into a flying fish. Thor and Redbeard noticed the flying fish and thought it was odd. They tried to catch it but it was too fast and slimy. Loki shape-shifted back to normal and they laughed.

Megan Currie (9)
Strath Of Appin Primary School, Appin

Run Quick

Everyone was screaming in the market so I ran home. My mum explained Vikings were invading Eforwic. They came and burnt my house down. My mum and I were so angry but we had to go! We found a boat. We sailed through the North Sea. It took days and days but finally we reached land! We wandered about and then we saw a gigantic treehouse! We tried climbing it but it went on and on forever. Finally we reached the top of the treehouse, we were in Asgard, home of the Viking gods. We stayed there forever.

Eve Lawrie (8)
Strath Of Appin Primary School, Appin

Rat In The Trenches

Hi, I'm Rat. I live in the trenches with my brother, Ratty. One day, me and Ratty were scavenging for food but the sergeant was hunting for rats. He saw us and he tried squishing us. We got away and scrambled into the sergeant's boot.

The next day me and Ratty went out looking for other rats. We had to go past the sergeant's camp. When we were just going past he stomped on Ratty and all that was left was a pile of blood. I ran home and was sad for a long time.

David Laughton (10)
Stromness Primary School, Stromness

The Soldier Who Wanted To Go Home

Ewan was a soldier in the trenches. 'It's time to go to bed.'

The next day Ewan woke up, well that's what he thought. He had not really woken up from his sleep. He was at his house, he thought he saw his family. He was still in the trenches. He got out of his bunk. He went to look at the countryside.

The next day was the day that Ewan got to go home. He was so excited to go home and get away from the trenches. Actually, it was a dream.

Eilidh Cursiter (9)
Stromness Primary School, Stromness

An Unusual Day

The 55th time out of the cave just double check if there are any human feet nearby. Nope! I'd better get out of the cave. That is one big footprint. Woah! There are so many of them and they all lead to… oh my gosh! A whole lair of humans and feet! This is awesome but scary at the same time. OK, maybe if I just walk backwards these humans won't wake up. That was a suggestion. OK, right, I'll just step backwards a little. Argh! Oh Mum! It's just you. Can you lead me home pretty please?

Sarah Loveridge (9)
Stromness Primary School, Stromness

It's A Trench Life

This is Alec, he's a soldier in WWI. This is his dog, Will, they're from London. This is their story.
'Blasted rats, go get them, Will.'
'Attention!' bellowed Sergeant Winston. Sergeant Winston was a tall and serious person. 'You, over there! Get on lookout!'
'Yes sir!'
'Everyone else with me. Ready. Aim. Fire!'
It was the same every day and they only had stale bread and watery stew to eat. Will was a great dog: he would catch rats and was very loyal and friendly. The only thing Alec could think about was, *when will the war end?*

Christy MacLeod (10)
Stromness Primary School, Stromness

No-Man's-Land

'Grenade!' Archie shouted and he dived out of the way.
Boom! 'Two can play at that game,' said Archie as he pulled the pin on his grenade and threw it with all his might.
In the distance Archie heard someone shouting, 'Grenade!' Thirty-nine German soldiers flew into the air, dead.
Archie started firing his gun and all the bullets stopped flying over his trench. Archie climbed over and went into No-Man's-Land. He looked around and thought to himself, *we've claimed No-Man's-Land at last.* Archie raised his fist in triumph and climbed into his trench.

Einar Towrie (10)
Stromness Primary School, Stromness

The Soldier And The Trench

This is a story all about a soldier named Richard. Richard lived in a trench with loads of other men. Oh how Richard longed to go home. Sadly he couldn't. Richard hated it in the trenches because you could easily get really bad foot rot, which Richard did *not* want to get!
One night, when everyone was getting into bed, Richard didn't. Instead, he climbed out of the trench and ran to the German trench and yelled, 'Oi! Why can't we just get along?'
'Erm? OK!'
'Well it worked out OK! So I guess that's the end of the war!'

Olivia Macnamara (9)
Stromness Primary School, Stromness

Bad Trenches

One day a soldier was writing in his diary. This was what he wrote…

I hate these trenches full of water, dirty and muddy. They're hateful, nobody likes them. People get foot rot and people miss their families worse than ever. It seems like we have been here for years but we have only been here for one. I just got told that my best friend died. Now I have to go on guard duty so I am ending here.

Alistair Park (9)
Stromness Primary School, Stromness

Another Day In The Trenches

In WWI there lived a British soldier called Thomas. He lived in the trenches. Thomas hated living in the trench, it was smelly and dirty and crawling with lice and mice. It was ten o'clock at night and Thomas was going on night duty with his friend, Jack. *Bang!* Thomas looked behind him and saw Jack, dead on the muddy ground. Thomas shouted, 'Everybody, get your guns ready!' Thomas saw them shooting then he started shooting. He looked behind him and about twenty men fell on the ground. Then Thomas said to himself, 'I hope this war ends very soon.'

Zara Johnston (9)
Stromness Primary School, Stromness

Left Behind

It was cold and rainy. I was thinking about my family. It was horrible in the trenches. Suddenly, I heard a noise, the Germans were attacking us! I got shot in my back, I fell down with a thud. I could hardly breathe. The British went out of the trenches and went away for war. They left me behind while I closed my eyes. The next day two British men found me and brought me home to my family. I felt I was in Heaven, being safely home with my wonderful family.

Matylda Kaluzinska (9)
Stromness Primary School, Stromness

The Most Scary Thing In The World

One day a soldier called Archie had the biggest fright of his life. Here's how: Archie was having a nap because he was very tired from fighting the night before. Then he heard a noise. It sounded like a humongous pack of hungry hippos. He ran to the sergeant and woke him. He said, 'Hey, there was a giant noise in the other trench.' But guess what? The sergeant didn't answer… he was dead. 'Oh no,' said Archie. Archie was so brave he ran and started fighting for his country. Then, all of a sudden, *bang!*

Leah Jean Hamilton (9)
Stromness Primary School, Stromness

The Rat Who Wanted Payback

There once was a rat called John. He lived in the trenches with all the soldiers. He was a nice rat until *pow!* Bill, his best friend, got whacked on the head with a spade. 'No!' said John. Bill went into a coma for days, then John saw a soldier holding a spade in his hand. 'He's the idiot who did it,' said John. 'Payback!' The soldier went to the supply room. John called all his mates to pick up the spade. He said, 'This is for Bill. Charge!' *Whack, whack, conk, kapow!*

Ethan Kennedy (9)
Stromness Primary School, Stromness

Stuck In The Trench

'I'm going out.'
'No! Don't go out, we're safe here.'
'I know but we need to fight them and win!'
'No, if you go out, I have to go with you because it's too dangerous.'
'Argh! My foot is stuck, I can't get out,' said Peter.
'Oh no, I think I'm stuck too. Help!'
'Help!' they both shouted.
'No one will hear us,' said Peter, 'they will be fighting already.'
'We will have to wait for them.'
'OK. Let's just try once more.' So they did and it worked. They were both fighting again with their army.

Kayla Swannie (10)
Stromness Primary School, Stromness

Lucky Men

I'm Mark... I wonder if I can get home? I better go to the planning room. 'Hey guys, let's think of a plan. Let's do it! Right, the enemy will be going for our medics so send twenty men there. Max, go defend the medics. Now Gonn, you go help.'
'The medics are good.'
'Okay, now we should be able to survive this war hopefully. Max, the enemy is on No-Man's-Land, it's Xmas… Wait! What?'
'They're singing. It's… it's…'
'I know! Silent Night!' So we sang too but the next day we won.

James Hogg (10)
Stromness Primary School, Stromness

A Night In The Trenches

One day two men named Joe and Jay had to go to war. Once they'd dug out a trench they went to bed. Once Jay woke up he saw that everyone was still asleep. 'That is weird, everyone is still asleep. Well I can wake them up later, right? Let's keep guard then… wait! What's that? Should I shoot?' *Bang!*
'Oh, it looks like you had a nightmare, man.'
'I must have. Well let's get back to sleep then.' That was his nightmare but will it come true?

Jordan Gunn (9)
Stromness Primary School, Stromness

The Bad Night Of Rain

Joe was trying to get to sleep in the day to get ready for the night. Joe's bedroom was underground. Joe shared a room with eight people. Joe was in his room reading when, *bang,* a massive explosion went off outside his room. Joe got hurt after a pile of dirt fell down and blocked the entrance. It was night now and Joe was still stuck in his room. Joe didn't know it was pouring with rain. Joe saw a mouse. The mouse was running around like mad. Now Joe and the mouse were digging upwards like mad people.

Leo Naylor (9)
Stromness Primary School, Stromness

Arthur's Diary

It has been four years since the war started and people are getting foot rot. I saw people shooting their arms and legs so they could go home. I want to go home but I need to protect my country. My name is Arthur. The weirdest thing that has happened was Christmas. We heard singing and knew the song, it was Silent Night. We joined in and said merry Christmas to them.
In the morning we went into No-Man's-Land. It didn't last. Before we knew it, we were shooting again. It was hard shooting them afterwards.

Katrina Braddock (10)
Stromness Primary School, Stromness

A Life Of A Soldier

One day a soldier was in the trenches. The Germans were shooting like mad at the trench. The soldier on sentry duty, called John, was calling for help so Jimmy and Arthur went to help John. When they got to the gun it was jammed and wouldn't shoot. None was an engineer so they called for one. There weren't any engineers so they had to un-jam it themselves. The bullet was really stuck and wouldn't go out so they made a run for the woods. When they'd run far they were lost.

Thorfinn Sinclair (9)
Stromness Primary School, Stromness

Bad Rat Day

Once upon a time there was a rat who was in the middle of nowhere. After a while, army men dug trenches! The rat was upset and the mouse as well. After a while lots of trenches were there. Rat never wanted war to happen, he hoped and hoped the war was going to end. It went on and on; it lasted for four years. It was horrible for the rat and mouse, to them it felt like forever. They only wanted peace to happen for them but it never came.

George Argo (10)
Stromness Primary School, Stromness

The Man Who Lived

One cold day James was in the trenches. The trenches were cold. James used his pistol to shoot. 'Yes, we got him,' said William. It was loud from all the other guns making noise. All around, other soldiers were shooting. They were surviving. James and William were beside each other when all of a sudden a German shot at James and William. Sadly they both died. One of their friends called their parents to tell their parents what'd happened. James and William were very brave to fight for their country.

Holly Mae McLellan (10)
Stromness Primary School, Stromness

The Soldiers In The Trenches

In 1914 some soldiers lived in trenches and got trenchfoot. One day they swapped around so the people in the trenches moved to the top of the trench for the night. Soon it was Christmas. 'Happy Christmas, Fritz.'
'Happy Christmas, Tommy.'
The next day war began again. Lots of people died. Just after Christmas they were fighting. They should have got to go home but they couldn't.
One day they got sent home with a medal and a medal was put on someone's hat which means they got injured in the war.

Taigan Adamson (9)
Stromness Primary School, Stromness

The Battle Of The Trenches

One day there was a soldier at home relaxing in bed. What was that? A rat? He quickly woke up with two beady eyes staring down at him. Startled, he quickly got to his feet, then it all came back to him: the gunshot, the bombing, the deaths and, worst of all… the trenches! Then he whacked the rat in the face with a shovel that they used to use to make the trenches. He heard some footsteps and *bam! Boing! Splat! Nibble!* An army of rats whacked him with a shovel and knocked him out cold…

Connor Bayliss (9)
Stromness Primary School, Stromness

Over The Top

Joe is a soldier in World War I in the trenches. Joe is on night watch. It was all quiet. Then, out of nowhere, they had to go over the top. His friend, Tom, was next to him. He was thinking about what'd happen if he died. *Bang!* Tom fell to the ground. 'No!' Joe started to shoot at the enemy. Joe shot a German dead. Joe was nearly in their trench. He jumped down into their trench, everyone was dead. Suddenly, someone yelled, 'Gas! Gas! Gas!' It was all silent in the trench. Would Joe survive or not?

Ewan Foubister (10)
Stromness Primary School, Stromness

Romance

Alex and Charlotte were on a rocky cliff that was abandoned because people thought that it was haunted. People would not go there to watch the sunset. Suddenly, the bit that Charlotte was standing on broke. Luckily, she grabbed onto a branch hanging from a tree. The branch split and she fell onto a rock. Alex rushed down to see if Charlotte was OK. Alex punched the number into the phone to call the emergency services. Just as they answered, the phone died.

Fern Dickson (8)
Tulloch Primary School, Perth

World War I

The guns were blazing as the bombs blew up. Aneena started to panic because Titan wasn't there with her. She wandered around while dodging bombs. The more she wandered the more she worried. She heard nothing but explosions and still, no sign of Titan. Suddenly, Aneena saw a man lying on the floor. Aneena went over to the man and she looked at his hurt face to find Titan dead on the ground. Aneena burst into tears; she realised he'd sacrificed himself for his country. She walked back and found out they'd won.

Milla Craig (9)
Tulloch Primary School, Perth

A Roaring Cave And Julius The Gladiator

I was a fierce gladiator who was wandering around Rome. I found a cave that had roaring coming from it. 'Curious,' I said and went into it with a fiery torch. I walked slowly into it. When I turned around there was a lion looking hungrily for a gladiator. The lion jumped up and scratched me but I started fighting it. I got my torch and swept it around but the lion was intelligent. I got my sword out and killed it. I got out safely and started wandering again, this time back home, walking very, very safely.

Elise Gavin (8)
Wallacestone Primary School, Falkirk

Gladiator Escape

I had woken up but I didn't know where I was. Then I felt the strong ropes that held my bruised hands together. I knew I needed to escape but I didn't know how. I heard footsteps coming down the deep, dark cavern. Then I saw who it was! 'Lunimious! What are you doing here?' I asked.
'I am here because I have captured you!' said Lunimious. Then I kicked him and a key flew from his clothes, through my ropes and into my lap. I then used the key to escape! I am so happy now!

Nathaniel Hutton (9)
Wallacestone Primary School, Falkirk

Surprise

Today, I am fighting against the Celts. We are losing! I am thinking about how we can win. I just saw a man who looks very strong. I'm going to ask him to join. 'What's your name?' I asked. 'Jeff,' said Jeff.

'Will you join the Roman army?' I asked.

'Yes,' answered Jeff.

I'm going back to base when I am attacked. Out of nowhere, Jeff came and punched them all. When we got back everywhere were Celts but I knew I was safe with Jeff. We started to fight. In the end we won the war!

Robbie Seaton (8)
Wallacestone Primary School, Falkirk

Allman's Break

Allman is stuck in a hot churning cage, sitting uncomfortably. After a few hours of sitting there, he thinks of making a clay key to get out. He climbs out, relieved to be out into the open. He finds himself in Rome outside a city. He goes inside and says, 'Hi!'

Seconds later, he's in court. Julius Caesar sits with some grapes. 'Zeb wa,' said Caesar.

Allman said, 'I wish Samsung phones were invented.'

'Get out,' said a furious Caesar.

He went out and said, 'Well, Rome isn't that good but what's Greece like?'

Euan Menzies (8)
Wallacestone Primary School, Falkirk

The Little Boys Who Fought Gladaitors

I woke up one night and went into my three sons' room. The one in the middle was called Anullana, the one on the right was called Norgott and the one on the left was called Digaray. They were gone. I didn't know where they'd gone but I was getting really worried. I went out into the street only I wasn't at my house, I was in the Colosseum. My boys were fighting! Somebody came up to me and took me away to a cage. I got scared. I heard something roaring. Please help me! Please come!

Carly Jane Crawford (8)
Wallacestone Primary School, Falkirk

The Warrior Of Rome

We had just conquered France. Even though we had won over France, we were forced to march on to Greece. We set up camp on a cliff, a few hundred miles from the gates of Athens. We were having a dinner of bread and milk then sleeping.
The next day I made my slave wash my feet, then we carried on the journey.
The next day we arrived at the gates. Then the war started. All I can remember is swords lashing and then I blacked out. When I woke up we had won and my leg and been chopped off.

Jack Savage (8)
Wallacestone Primary School, Falkirk

Gladiator

One day Jeff was walking down the street, thinking about his next gladiator fight. Suddenly, an evil goddess named Anxious appeared and tried to kill him with a fireball. However, she missed because Jeff outpaced her. Anxious disappeared but nobody knows where she went. Jeff quickly went to tell the emperor. When he arrived at the emperor's palace he had already been murdered by Anxious!

Kailim Grant (8)
Wallacestone Primary School, Falkirk

The Great Escape

After a long day Gordon went to sleep. Queen Boudicca snuck in his room and kidnapped him. When he woke up he was trapped in a cage, surrounded by the Iceni tribe who had grumpy faces. Only one had a happy face. That guy was called Daz. Daz was always so nice to visitors, he actually helped people that the Iceni tribe captured. He was never a true member. At lunch he made a key out of Play-Doh (let's just say you could do that). He unlocked the cage. Gordon was free! 'Bye-bye. See you later, bye!'

Olivia Chomczuk (8)
Wallacestone Primary School, Falkirk

The Good Lion

One day a lonely rich lady was eating fruit but suddenly a flicker of a light went and the soldiers were grabbing on to her. 'Leave me alone.'
'No! We are taking you to the dungeon.'
'Why?'
'Because we want to take over the world.'
After that she was trapped in the dungeon with rats.
The next day a lion came. She was scared but then she learnt it was friendly. It released her and they both ran. She said to the lion, 'Are you my friend?'
The lion replied, 'Yes.' They defeated the soldiers. Lilly finally had a friend.

Beth Fletcher (8)
Wallacestone Primary School, Falkirk

The Dungeon

One time I woke up in a different bed in a dungeon in the middle of nowhere. I had no idea where I was. I heard lots of weird noises and suddenly a giant lion came and rattled on the bars. I felt terrified that I would die: I was only eight years old with a lion about to eat me! I decided I would try to sleep but with the lion roaring it was almost impossible to get to sleep. Finally, the lion simmered down and I drifted off. So did the lion. Wow! That was really, really close!

Cameron McLean (8)
Wallacestone Primary School, Falkirk

A War Between Scottish And Romans

Once there was a debate in beautiful Rome between the Romans and the Scottish. Then the Scottish came. Rome barricaded its doors. When the Scottish came it was midnight. They bashed through the gate. Unfortunately, they had cannons but the Romans had archers with flame-throwers, then they sent out the lions. But the Scots had a wizard with firebolts. Rome sent out boulders to crush the cannons. Then the Scots retreated. The Emperor said, 'Move out.' The Romans found a village and camped outside it. Then the Emperor said, 'This is war. Now we shall move upon Scotland.'

Lewis Smith (8)
Wallacestone Primary School, Falkirk

Dean And The Lion

A man was put in prison. He was put in prison. He was beginning to get out but nobody would listen. He bribed a Roman soldier. Suddenly, a lion appeared and killed all of the soldiers. Dean and the lion escaped together. Dean jumped onto the lion's back and ran quickly to the middle of nowhere. They dug a large hole underground and hid inside forever.

Dean Johnston (9)
Wallacestone Primary School, Falkirk

Colto's Small Adventure

Colto is very lost. When he was two, his parents got kidnapped and he became a slave. Now he's seventeen and still a slave. He has woken up in the middle of nowhere. He stands up and looks around. There were two houses. He went into the first one.
'Hello,' said the guy at the door.
'Who lives in the other house?' asked Colto.
'Mr and Mrs Toot,' said the man.
Colto paused. Toot was his second name. He rushed to the other house. Mrs Toot opened the door. 'Son!' shouted Mrs Toot, cuddling Colto.

Cameron Hudson (8)
Wallacestone Primary School, Falkirk

The Clumsy Gladiator

One day, a gladiator was having a fight but the gladiator was extremely clumsy. He had lost his last ten games and he was already making mistakes. He was swinging his sword everywhere like a horse. The emperor was watching in disgust. After the match the emperor said he was going to execute him. He thought that was too harsh! There was no escape.
The next day it was time to die! Over one hundred people were there to see him but there was a gap in the crowd and he wasn't chained! He escaped, amazingly!

Robbie Hill (8)
Wallacestone Primary School, Falkirk

The Dungeon

A soldier called Lanis was a very brave soldier. One day he woke up alone and… he was in a dungeon! He saw a lion. The lion was fierce, Lanis didn't know what to do. He was very scared but then he saw the guard. The guard was asleep, so Lanis made a hook out of hay. He got the key but the lion was chasing him. He was very scared, but needed to get home too. Then, he saw his family looking for him. They all got home safely.

Eva Inglis (8)
Wallacestone Primary School, Falkirk

Locked Life Of A Roman Empress

One day, me and my wife were walking along the temple path and I was knocked out by a mean man. When I woke up I had lost my wife, she had been kidnapped! Now I am in a cage, I am making a key out of this clay but I don't think there's enough. 'Yup, I am right: no clay!' The robber knew I was smart. 'Oh wait, Garin will save me! Right? Oh… wait… he was knocked out by an iron bar. I'll find my own way. Hey, he's coming for my dinner! This is my chance. Yes!'

Finlay Christie (8)
Wallacestone Primary School, Falkirk

Years of YoungWriters

YOUNG WRITERS
INFORMATION

We hope you have enjoyed reading this book – and that you will continue to in the coming years.

If you're a young writer who enjoys reading and creative writing, or the parent of an enthusiastic poet or story writer, do visit our website www.youngwriters.co.uk. Here you will find free competitions, workshops and games, as well as recommended reads, a poetry glossary and our blog.

If you would like to order further copies of this book, or any of our other titles give us a call or visit **www.youngwriters.co.uk**.

Young Writers
Remus House
Coltsfoot Drive
Peterborough
PE2 9BF

(01733) 890066
info@youngwriters.co.uk